"Undoubtedly i[...]
make her wec[...]a."
He paused, and the air between them
seemed to tremble. "But there is another
reason why I want you to stay."

His voice was as deep and soft as crushed velvet.
Belle's heart jerked painfully against her ribs
and she watched, paralyzed, as his head slowly
lowered and the moonlight was obscured. She
licked her dry lips with the tip of her tongue.

"What...reason?" she whispered.

"This..."

Loukas brushed his mouth over hers, capturing
her surprised gasp as her lips parted helplessly.

CHANTELLE SHAW lives on the Kent coast, five minutes from the sea, and does much of her thinking about the characters in her books while walking on the beach. An avid reader from an early age, she found that school friends used to hide their books when she visited, but Chantelle would retreat into her own world, and she still writes stories in her head all the time.

Chantelle has been blissfully married to her own tall, dark and very patient hero for over twenty years and has six children. She began to read Harlequin® romance novels as a teenager, and throughout the years of being a stay-at-home mum to her brood, she found romance fiction helped her to stay sane! Her aim is to write books that provide an element of escapism, fun and of course romance for the countless women who juggle work and a home life and who need their precious moments of "me" time. She enjoys reading and writing about strong-willed, feisty women and even stronger-willed sexy heroes. Chantelle is at her happiest when writing. She is particularly inspired while cooking dinner, which unfortunately results in a lot of culinary disasters! She also loves gardening, taking her very badly behaved terrier for walks and eating chocolate (followed by more walking—at least the dog is slim!).

Other titles by Chantelle Shaw available in ebook

Harlequin Presents® Extra

142—UNTOUCHED UNTIL MARRIAGE
165—HIS UNKNOWN HEIR
182—A DANGEROUS INFATUATION

AFTER THE GREEK AFFAIR

CHANTELLE SHAW

~ After Hours with the Greek ~

Harlequin®

TORONTO NEW YORK LONDON
AMSTERDAM PARIS SYDNEY HAMBURG
STOCKHOLM ATHENS TOKYO MILAN MADRID
PRAGUE WARSAW BUDAPEST AUCKLAND

Recycling programs
for this product may
not exist in your area.

ISBN-13: 978-0-373-52866-0

AFTER THE GREEK AFFAIR

First North American Publication 2012

AFTER THE GREEK AFFAIR

CHAPTER ONE

BELLE ANDERSEN extracted her mobile phone from her handbag and skimmed the text message she had received from Larissa Christakis, explaining how to reach her brother Loukas's private Greek island.

> As I'm getting married on Aura, it would be wonderful if you could come to the island to work on the designs for my dress so that you can get a feel for the setting. You can catch the ferry from the port of Lavrion in Athens to the island of Kea. Let me know what time you plan to arrive and I'll make sure a boat is waiting to bring you to Aura.

The ferry had arrived at Kea ten minutes ago and the last of the passengers were disembarking. Further along the quay several fishing boats rocked gently on a cobalt sea that reflected the cloudless blue sky above. The little port of Korissia was a picturesque place. Square white houses with terracotta-coloured roofs lined the harbour and gleamed brilliantly in the sunshine, and behind them green hills swathed in a profusion of brightly coloured wild flowers rose in graceful curves.

Belle's artistic eye appreciated the beauty of her surroundings, but after a four-hour flight to Athens and another hour on the ferry to Kea she was looking forward to reaching her destination. Perhaps one of the fishing boats had been sent to collect her, she thought, lifting her hand to shield her eyes from the sun as she stared along the quay. A group of fishermen were standing around chatting but no one paid her any attention. The other passengers from the ferry had dispersed into the town. With a sigh she picked up her suitcases and began to walk towards the fishermen.

The May sunshine was blissfully warm after the grey, unseasonably chilly London Belle had left behind. Her lips twitched when she recalled her brother Dan's reaction to the news that she would be spending the next week in Greece while he remained on their old houseboat on the Thames, which had sprung a leak.

'Spare me a thought while you're hob-nobbing with a Greek billionaire on his paradise island, won't you?' Dan had teased. 'While you're topping up your tan I'll be patching up the boat—yet again—before I head off to Wales for a photo shoot.'

'I'll be working, not lazing in the sun,' Belle had pointed out. 'And I don't suppose I'll have much to do with Loukas Christakis. Larissa told me her brother spends much of his time at his company's offices in Athens, or visiting his many business projects around the world. Even the date of Larissa's wedding was determined by Loukas's schedule. Apparently the last week in June is the only time he has free.'

A frown wrinkled Belle's brow as she continued along the quay. During her conversations with Larissa the Greek girl had frequently mentioned her brother, and it was clear she adored him. But Belle had gained the impression that Loukas Christakis was a man who was used to having his own way, and she suspected that Larissa was slightly in awe of him.

The very fact that she had been asked to design and make Larissa's wedding dress, as well as dresses for her two bridesmaids, in five weeks rather than the six months she would usually expect the commission to take was due in part to Loukas, Belle mused. Of course he was not responsible for the fact that the first designer his sister had commissioned had suffered some sort of personal crisis and disappeared—Larissa had been rather vague about the details of what had happened— but Loukas's insistence that the wedding should still go ahead at the end of June as planned must have put Larissa under enormous pressure. She had been close to tears when she had visited the Wedding Belle studio a week ago, and clearly relieved when Belle had assured her that she could make her a dress in time.

Her frown deepened as she recalled the tremor in Larissa's voice when she had explained that she needed Belle to come to Aura and begin working on designs for the dress as quickly as possible. She hadn't even met Loukas Christakis yet, but she instinctively disliked him, Belle thought with a grimace.

She gave herself a mental shake. It wasn't fair to allow her dislike of domineering John Townsend—the man she had grown up believing to be her father—to colour her judgement of all other men. Larissa's brother was probably charming. Certainly enough women seemed to think so, if the reports in the gossip columns about his energetic love-life with a bevy of beautiful mistresses were to be believed.

A flash of movement far out to sea caught her eye and she halted and watched a speedboat streaking towards the harbour, churning up twin trails of white froth in its wake. It slowed as it approached the quay, the low throb of its engine shattering the quiet. Sleek and powerful, the boat was eye-catching, but it was the man at the wheel who trapped Belle's gaze and caused her heart to jolt beneath her ribs.

When Larissa had said someone would pick her up from Kea and bring her to Aura it hadn't crossed Belle's mind that that someone might be Loukas Christakis himself. The pictures she'd seen of him in newspapers and magazines did not do him justice, she thought dazedly. Sure, the photographs had faithfully recorded the thick jet-black hair swept back from his brow, his chiselled features, square jaw and the innately sensual curve of his mouth. But a photo could not capture his aura of raw power, the magnetism that demanded attention and made it impossible to look away from him.

'Are you Belle Andersen?' His accented voice was deep and gravelly and so intensely male that the tiny hairs all over Belle's body stood on end. Heat surged through her and her skin suddenly seemed acutely sensitive, so that she was aware of the faint abrasion of her lacy bra brushing against her nipples.

'Y…yes…' To her embarrassment the word emerged as a strangled croak. Her heart-rate quickened as she watched him steer the boat broadside against the harbour wall, and throw a rope around a bollard before he jumped onto the quay.

'I'm Loukas Christakis,' he announced, striding towards her. Supremely confident and self-assured, he moved with surprising grace for such a big man. He was well over six feet tall, Belle estimated, and narrow-hipped, his long legs encased in faded denims that moulded his powerful thighs. Through his close-fitting black tee shirt she could see the delineation of his abdominal muscles, and the shirt's vee-shaped neckline revealed an expanse of bronzed skin and wiry black chest hair.

Dear heaven, he was something else! Belle swallowed. Never in her life had she felt so overwhelmingly aware of a man. Her heart was racing and her palms felt damp. She wanted to speak, make some banal remark about the weather and break the tension that gripped her, but her mouth felt dry and her brain seemed to have stopped functioning. She wished he wasn't wearing sunglasses. Perhaps if she could see his eyes he would seem less imposing, although somehow she doubted it.

Professionalism finally came to her rescue and she held out her hand to him, thankful that her voice sounded normal as she murmured, 'I'm pleased to meet you, Mr Christakis. Larissa spoke of you when she visited my studio in London.'

Was it her imagination, or was there was an infinitesimal pause before he grasped her fingers in a brief handshake? His grip was firm, and once again she was conscious of his power and strength. He towered over her, his big body silhouetted against the bright sunlight, and unbidden she found herself wondering what it would be like to be crushed against his broad chest.

He released her hand, but to her surprise instead of stepping away from her he took hold of her arm. 'I am delighted to meet you too, Ms Andersen.' The greeting was perfunctory, and Belle detected a faint edge of impatience in his tone. 'I need to speak to you. Shall we find somewhere to sit down?'

Without waiting for her to reply he picked up the larger of her suitcases, slid his hand beneath her elbow and steered her across the road to a bar, where tables were set beneath a striped awning. Belle struggled to keep up with his long stride in her three-inch heels. She felt like a recalcitrant child being dragged along by an impatient parent and she glared at him indignantly, but before she could say a word he pulled out a chair and she found herself guided firmly down onto it.

No doubt tourists found it a charming place to spend an idle hour watching the boats in the harbour, she thought with a frown when Loukas rounded the table and lowered himself into the seat opposite her. But *she* had come to Greece to work and she was eager make a start.

'Mr Christakis—'

'Would you like a drink?' A waiter materialised at their table, and without waiting for her response Loukas spoke to the youth in rapid Greek. The only word Belle understood was *retsina*, which she knew was a Greek wine.

'Make that a fruit juice for me, thank you,' she said quickly.

The waiter glanced at Loukas—almost as if seeking permission to bring her the drink she had ordered, Belle thought irritably. She checked her watch and saw that it was eight hours since she had left home that morning. She felt hot, dishevelled, and in no mood to pander to a man with an oversized ego. 'Mr Christakis, I don't actually want a drink,' she said crisply. 'What I would like is to go straight to Aura. Your sister has commissioned me to design her wedding dress, and with a deadline of just over a month it is imperative that I start work immediately.'

'Yes…' Loukas lifted his hand to remove his sunglasses and subjected Belle to a cool appraisal. 'That's what I want to talk to you about.'

His eyes were the colour of flint, hard and uncompromising. Disappointment swooped inside Belle when she noted the distinct lack of welcome in his expression. What on earth had made her think that her intense awareness of him was reciprocated? she asked herself impatiently. Even more ridiculous was the notion that she wished it was. She frantically blanked out the thought and forced herself to meet his gaze, conscious of the uneven thud of her heart as she studied his heavy black brows, his strong nose and full-lipped mouth. The shadow of dark stubble on his jaw only added to his blatant sex appeal.

What would it feel like to have that sensual mouth move over hers, at first in a leisurely tasting, and then crushing her lips beneath his in hungry passion? She was shocked as much by the clarity of the image in her head as by her wayward thoughts, and felt the heat rise in her cheeks.

Loukas's eyes narrowed and his gaze became speculative. Had he guessed what she had been thinking? Mortified, she felt her blush deepen. Everything about him—from the proud angle of his head to his relaxed, almost insolent air as he trailed his eyes over her—exuded arrogance. No doubt he was used to the effect he had on women, Belle thought dismally, wishing the ground would swallow her up.

* * *

Life seemed to be doing its damnedest at the moment to be difficult, Loukas brooded irritably as he stared at the woman opposite him, watching the flush of soft colour stain her cheeks. It should have been a simple matter to inform Belle Andersen that there had been a change of plan and she was no longer required to design his sister's wedding dress, hand her a hefty cheque to cover her expenses, and then see her onto the next ferry back to Athens. Instead he found himself transfixed by a pair of cornflower-blue eyes, fringed by long hazel lashes and shadowed by an air of vulnerability that he found intriguing.

He had not expected her to be so beautiful. Even more surprising was his reaction to her, Loukas acknowledged. He spent his life surrounded by beautiful women. He was a connoisseur who dated top models and glamorous socialites, and he preferred tall, willowy, sophisticated types. Belle was a tiny, doll-like creature, but from the moment he had seen her standing on the quay his attention had been riveted—and now he could not tear his eyes from her exquisite face.

Her features were perfect: those startling blue eyes, a neat little nose, high cheekbones, and a soft pink mouth that was undeniably tempting. Her hair was hidden from view beneath her wide-brimmed hat, but he would lay a bet that with her pale, almost Nordic skin tone she was a blonde. The cream hat with black trim was the perfect accessory for her expertly tailored skirt and jacket. Black patent stiletto heels and handbag completed her outfit.

He wondered if her elegant 1950s-inspired suit was one of her own creations. If so, then perhaps he was worrying unnecessarily about her suitability to design

Larissa's wedding dress? He entertained the thought briefly and then dismissed it. Belle Andersen was an unknown quantity. The company search he had made on the internet the previous night, after Larissa had sprung the news that she had chosen a new designer to make her wedding dress, had revealed that the bridalwear company Wedding Belle had barely made a profit in the previous financial year and had little capital. In other words Belle's company was struggling financially—just as Demakis Designs, whom Larissa had first commissioned to make her dress, had been.

Loukas blamed himself for the fact that his sister did not have a wedding dress five weeks before her wedding. If only he had checked out Toula Demakis he would have discovered that the Greek designer had serious financial problems and that her business was on the verge of bankruptcy. But he had been abroad when Larissa had appointed Toula, and had been unaware that his trusting sister had paid the wretched woman the entire cost of her dress in advance.

That had been six months ago, and as the date of the wedding had drawn nearer Toula Demakis had made increasingly wild excuses to explain the delay in completing the dress—excuses which unfortunately Larissa had not relayed to him until the unscrupulous designer had disappeared with the money.

Perhaps he was to blame that his sister was so unworldly? Loukas thought heavily. But she meant the world to him. He had acted as a surrogate father to her for most of her life, and maybe he was a little overprotective of her. With the wedding looming, he had decided to take charge of the situation and had asked his friend, internationally acclaimed fashion designer

Jacqueline Jameson, to make Larissa's dress—unaware until last night that Larissa had already appointed a new designer.

Perhaps it was unfair to be suspicious of Ms Andersen just because Toula Demakis had turned out to be a dishonest crook, Loukas conceded. But unlike his sister he never trusted anyone—a lesson he had learned the hard way, and which had proved invaluable in both his business and private life. Maybe the English designer *was* totally reliable, but the wedding was fast approaching and he was not prepared to risk Larissa being let down again.

He leaned back in his seat and studied Belle's delicate features. She was exceptionally attractive, he acknowledged. But he did not need to remind himself that his sister was his only consideration. His unexpected attraction to Belle Andersen was inconsequential, and he was confident that he would have forgotten her within minutes of escorting her onto the ferry. It was a pity, though, Loukas mused, feeling a sharp stab of desire in his groin. Under different circumstances he would not have wasted a moment seducing her into his bed…

Belle wished that Loukas Christakis would stop staring at her. She could feel herself growing increasingly flustered, and when their drinks were served she gulped down her fruit juice simply because holding the glass to her lips provided a welcome distraction from his disturbing presence.

'You were thirsty after all,' he commented dryly.

She flushed, remembering that she had told him she did not want a drink. 'I've been travelling all day,' she said pointedly.

Cool grey eyes trapped hers. 'I appreciate that—just as I appreciate that the last thing you will want to hear now is that your journey has been unnecessary. But I'm afraid I have to inform you that my sister has chosen another designer to make her wedding dress and no longer requires your services.'

For a few seconds Belle stared at him in dumbstruck silence while his words sank in. 'But…'

'I hope this will recompense you for your travel expenses and time,' Loukas continued smoothly, opening his wallet and handing her a slip of paper.

Numbly, Belle took the cheque. The figure scrawled in black ink covered her travel costs a hundred times over, but it did nothing to alleviate her feeling of sick disappointment. 'I don't understand,' she said slowly. 'I received a text message from Larissa only yesterday, saying how excited she was that I was going to design her dress and that she was looking forward to my arrival. Are you saying she's changed her mind since then?'

This time she was sure she had not imagined Loukas's slight hesitation before he spoke, but his voice was level and even politely apologetic as he murmured, 'I'm afraid so.'

Belle did not know what to say. She felt winded, as if someone had punched her and forced all the air from her lungs. She was stunned by the news that Larissa had had a change of heart. She stared down at the cheque, her vision suddenly blurred.

It was ridiculous to cry, she told herself fiercely. But this was to have been her big chance. Larissa's wedding was *the* society wedding of the year.

Loukas Christakis was one of the richest men in Greece; recent reports suggested that he had moved up to billionaire status—which was an astounding achievement considering that he had been born into poverty. He was regarded as a national hero in his own country and a celebrity in the US, where he had started his property development empire. Everyone who was anyone had been invited to the marriage of his only sister.

'I've never met half the people on the guest list,' Larissa had confided to Belle. 'If I'm honest I would have been happy with a smaller affair. But I know Loukas is determined to make my wedding the most memorable day of my life and so I feel I can't complain.'

The commission to design the bride's dress for such a high profile wedding had been guaranteed to give Wedding Belle huge media attention. Belle knew it could have been the making of her fledgling business, bringing in new orders and providing a vital lifeline when the bank was threatening to call in her loan.

But her disappointment was due to more than a lost business opportunity, she thought bleakly. She had taken an instant liking to Larissa, and had felt deeply sympathetic when she'd heard how the Greek girl had been let down by her first designer. In London, Larissa had excitedly pored over Belle's portfolio, and had rummaged among the samples of vintage French lace, marabou feathers and other trimmings like a child in a sweetshop. Her enthusiasm had been infectious—so what had happened between then and now to cause her to choose a different designer? It didn't make sense, Belle brooded. Something did not feel right.

She frowned as she recalled something Larissa had said when she had visited the Wedding Belle studio. *'Loukas wants Jacqueline Jameson to make my dress.'*

She'd recognised the name, of course. Jacqueline Jameson was a favourite designer of celebrities across the globe, and at least four Hollywood actresses had worn her dresses to last year's most prestigious film awards. Belle had felt flattered when Larissa had insisted that she wanted to get married in a Belle Andersen creation, but it seemed that at the last minute she had changed her mind—*or given in to her brother.*

She stared suspiciously at the arrogant features of the man sitting opposite her, noting the hard line of his jaw and the glint of steel in his eyes. Had Loukas got his own way? Had he put pressure on his sister to employ the designer of *his* choice? From what Larissa had told her it sounded as though Loukas had hijacked the wedding and was determined to turn it into a showcase to demonstrate his wealth and success, so it followed that he would want Larissa to pick an internationally acclaimed designer to make her dress.

There was only one way to find out exactly what was going on, and that was to ask Larissa, Belle decided, opening her handbag and taking out her phone.

Across the table she was aware that Loukas no longer looked relaxed, but had tensed and was watching her intently. 'You need to make a call right now?' he queried, his heavy brows drawing together.

'I had an arrangement with your sister,' she informed him, relieved that she sounded so calm when her insides were churning. 'I'd just like to check with Larissa that she is happy with her decision to commission another designer instead of me.' She hesitated, and felt a little shiver run down her spine when her eyes clashed with his hard grey gaze. 'Assuming that Larissa *did* actually make that decision and it wasn't made for her.'

CHAPTER TWO

'IT ISN'T necessary to involve my sister.'

Belle gasped as Loukas reached across the table and plucked her phone from her hand. She made a wild grab for it, but he was too quick for her and held it out of her reach, unperturbed by her furious glare.

'How dare you? Give that back. What do you mean, it's not necessary to involve Larissa? Surely she is the one person who *should* be involved? This is about what *she* wants, after all—or have you forgotten that fact?' she said sharply.

Loukas's eyes narrowed at her tone. Many years ago he had been a poor immigrant, living in one of the most deprived areas of New York, but now he was a billionaire business tycoon and he was used to being treated with deference by everyone he met. He did not appreciate having his head snapped off by a diminutive English dressmaker whose business was hanging by a thread.

'I know what is best for my sister—and with respect, Ms Andersen, I'm pretty sure that person is not you,' he said bluntly.

Belle blinked at him, shocked by his arrogant assumption that he knew his sister's mind better than Larissa did herself. But why was she surprised? she wondered. Loukas Christakis had a reputation as a ruthless individual who had fought his way to the top and had no compunction about trampling on anyone who got in his way.

He was watching her with a calculating, predatory look in his slate-grey eyes that was unnerving. But Belle had spent too many years being bossed around by the man she was glad she no longer had to call her father; she had finally broken free of John Townsend and she refused to be intimidated by any man.

'Larissa hasn't changed her mind, has she?' she challenged him fiercely. '*You've* decided you want Jacqueline Jameson to make her dress. But why? Have you ever *seen* any of my dresses? Why are you so certain that I can't make Larissa the perfect wedding gown she's hoping for?'

Loukas's jaw tightened at Belle's belligerent tone, but to his annoyance his conscience pricked. She had a point. 'No, I haven't seen any of your work,' he admitted.

Despite her anger at his attitude, Belle found her eyes drawn to his broad shoulders. He must work out, she thought, feeling a tightening sensation in the pit of her stomach when she lowered her gaze to his well-defined biceps. His skin was a deep bronze colour and his forearms were covered in fine black hairs. What would it feel like to have those strong, muscular arms around her? whispered the little voice in her head that seemed hell-bent on unsettling her.

She suddenly realised that Loukas was speaking again and hastily forced her mind away from his undeniably sexy body.

'But you're right; I *would* prefer Jacqueline to design Larissa's dress. She is a personal friend as well as an internationally acclaimed designer. I've never heard of *you*,' he said bluntly. 'All I know is that Wedding Belle has only existed for three years. To be frank, I'm not sure you have the experience to design a top-quality wedding dress for my sister and complete the commission to such a tight deadline. Jacqueline has run her design company for twenty years, and I know I can trust her to produce a stunning bridal gown in time for the wedding.'

'*I* can do that—if only you would give me the chance.' Belle leaned forward, her eyes fixed on Loukas. 'I'm prepared to work night and day to ensure that Larissa has her dream dress.' When his harsh expression did not alter she shook her head in frustration. 'Larissa chose *me*. Surely that counts for something? She's an adult who should be free to make her own decisions. What right do you have to organise her life for her?'

'My sister has already been let down by the first designer she chose. Having spent days trying to console her when the wedding dress she had been promised never materialised, I think I have every right to ensure she is not disappointed again,' Loukas snapped. 'I realise you must have hoped that this commission would benefit your business, but I have paid you a substantial fee for your wasted time today.'

Belle's eyes dropped to the slip of paper in her hand. 'So this cheque is actually a bribe?' she said in an appalled voice. She hadn't understood why Loukas had given her enough money to pay for a luxury world cruise rather than simply reimburse her for her plane ticket to Greece, but it made sense now. 'You expect me to take the money and disappear back to England. Larissa will have no choice at this late stage but to agree to

Jacqueline Jameson making her dress, and you'll have your own way. My God!' She stared at him disgustedly. 'What are you? Some kind of control freak?'

The crack of Loukas's palm onto the wooden table was as loud as a gunshot and caused Belle almost to jump out of her skin. 'I refuse to apologise for wanting to protect my sister,' he growled, his face taut with anger. 'She trusted Toula Demakis, but all the damned woman was interested in was getting as much money as she could out of her. Now the wedding is five weeks away, and I am not prepared to risk Larissa being let down again.'

Belle's heart sank when she saw the implacable expression on Loukas's face. 'It's true that Wedding Belle isn't doing as well as I'd hoped when I started out,' she admitted honestly. 'But many businesses are struggling because of the economic recession.'

She had been so excited three years ago when, soon after graduating from art school, she had used the small inheritance from her mother to pay the first year's rent on the studio. Not even John's scathing comment that she did not stand a chance in the cut-throat world of fashion design had dented her optimism. She hadn't cared about his opinion. The revelation that he was not her father had freed her from his tyranny and she no longer had to put up with him trying to control her life.

Why did some men feel the need to exert their power? she wondered, darting a glance at Loukas's arrogant features. He had said he wanted to protect his sister, but it seemed to Belle that—like John Townsend—Loukas had a pig-headed desire always to have his own way. There seemed little point in trying to persuade him to listen to her, she thought wearily. But the memory of

Larissa's excitement when she had visited the studio in London prompted her to try.

'I can't deny that a high-profile wedding could do wonders for my business. But that's not why I want to make Larissa's dress.' She ignored Loukas's sceptical expression and leaned across the table, an intent expression on her face. 'I love what I do. Making wedding dresses isn't just a job, it's my passion, and even if Larissa's wedding was going to be a small affair, with only a handful of guests and no media interest, I'd still be glad that she chose me as her designer.'

She tore the cheque in half and pushed the pieces across the table towards him. 'I'm not interested in your money. I want to design Larissa's dress because I like her. We clicked instantly when she came to my studio, and I'm excited about showing her my ideas.'

She met his steel-grey gaze unflinchingly, honesty and a fierce determination to convince him that she was genuine blazing in her eyes. 'Give me a chance, Mr Christakis, and I promise I won't let your sister down.'

Her eyes were the cerulean blue of the sky on a summer's day, Loukas noted. His attention was locked on her lovely face, as if he was in the grip of a sorcerer's spell and could not look away from her. He was utterly fascinated by her animated features when she spoke, the way she moved her hands in quick, darting gestures to emphasise a point. She reminded him of a beautiful, fragile butterfly—like the ones that often settled on the bougainvillaea bushes growing over the walls of his villa—and he was sure that if he tried to capture her she would fly away and evade him.

Why was he indulging in such fanciful nonsense?

he asked himself irritably. He was captivated by Belle Andersen—drawn by some invisible force to lean forward across the table so that his face was inches from hers. She had spoken of passion for her work, but the word evoked an image in his head of her lying on his bed, her slender body naked, her face flushed and her incredible blue eyes darkened with desire.

Her skin was as smooth as porcelain, her soft pink lips—slightly parted, he noted—a temptation he was struggling to resist. The atmosphere between them simmered with sexual tension, and the voices of the other customers in the bar faded and did not impinge on his ferocious awareness of her.

'Are you married, Ms Andersen?'

Belle blinked, the sound of Loukas's voice releasing her from the enchantment of his mesmerising sensuality so that she was once more aware of her surroundings. She heard the clink of glasses as a waiter passed by their table, the cry of a gull strutting along the quay.

Dear heaven! She closed her eyes briefly and dragged oxygen into her lungs, her heart hammering. For a few heart-stopping seconds she had thought that Loukas was going to kiss her. His face was so close to hers that when he spoke his breath whispered across her lips, and she imagined him closing the gap between them and slanting his mouth over hers. She felt almost bereft that he had not.

'No…no, I'm not,' she mumbled, finding herself reluctant to sit back in her seat and break the tangible, indefinable *something* that quivered in the air between them. 'Why do you ask?'

'I wondered whether your *passion*…' he hesitated fractionally, his eyes lingering on her mouth '…for designing wedding gowns stems from your own experience as a bride.'

Belle shook her head firmly. 'My passion is for art and creativity. I am inspired by history. At the moment I'm especially influenced by the sumptuous extravagance of the Palace of Versailles at the time of Louis XIV. The château is renowned as one of the most stunning examples of eighteenth-century French art. I've visited several times and come away with ideas that I've incorporated into my designs. My aspiration is to transform the images in my head and make dresses that are incredibly beautiful, yet wearable. I think a bride needs to feel comfortable on her big day and confident that her dress works on a practical level—'

She broke off and gave a rueful smile when she realised that she had been talking non-stop. 'There you are,' she said sheepishly, embarrassed by a display of enthusiasm that she was sure made her sound like a gauche teenager rather than a professional businesswoman. 'I'm afraid I tend to get carried away by my passion.'

In the silence that followed her words she was aware of the tension that smouldered like glowing embers between her and Loukas, ready to catch light at any moment. Her senses seemed to be attuned to him, so that she was conscious of the faint acceleration of his breathing and the subtle scent of his cologne. Her heart-rate quickened and she could feel her cheeks grow warm, as if molten heat was coursing through her veins. What was the matter with her? she asked herself angrily. She had met attractive men before. But none had ever made such an impact on her as Loukas Christakis.

Belle's passion for her designing was undeniable, Loukas brooded, unable to tear his eyes from her lovely face. Maybe he should he forget his reservations about employing an unknown designer and trust Larissa's judgement?

'How did my sister come to hear of you?' he asked abruptly.

'She saw some of my dresses featured in the fashion magazine *Style Icon*.'

Loukas's brows rose in surprise. 'You must be more well-known than I thought if your work caught the attention of the editor of *Style Icon*. The magazine is reputed to be the world's top-selling fashion bible.'

'Well, it was a bit of luck, really,' Belle explained honestly. 'My brother was working on a wedding shoot for the magazine. You might have heard of him? Dan Townsend? He's making quite a name for himself as a fashion photographer. When one of the designers dropped out at the last minute, Dan persuaded the editor of *Style Icon* to use some dresses from my collection.'

Against his will Loukas found himself intrigued by Belle. Her personal life was of no interest to him, he reminded himself, yet for some inexplicable reason he wanted to know more about her. 'Why do you and your brother have different names?'

Belle hesitated. There was no shame in admitting the truth, she reminded herself. The fact that she was illegitimate was not her fault. It had been her choice to change her surname by deed poll from Townsend to her mother's maiden name of Andersen when she had discovered the truth of her identity.

'We have different fathers.'

It was the one thing that had saddened her when she had learned that John was not her biological father. But Dan had insisted it did not matter. 'You're still my sister, even if technically we're only half-siblings,' he had told her gently. 'And look on the bright side—at least you're not related to the most unpleasant man on the planet. I have to live with the knowledge that because Mum chose to remain married to my father you never knew *your* father.'

Nor would she ever know now. Her mother had died and taken the identity of the man she had had an affair with to her grave, Belle thought sadly. She had no way of finding out who her real father was, although she had thought about him endlessly during the past three years—since John had made his stunning revelation on the day of her mother's funeral that she was not his daughter.

If only Gudrun had told her the truth... She quickly blocked off that pathway of thought. It was pointless to feel angry with her mother, ridiculous to feel betrayed by the woman she had adored. Gudrun had obviously believed she was doing the right thing when she had allowed Belle to grow up believing that John Townsend was her father.

But her mother had been forced to make a stark choice, Belle acknowledged. She knew now that John had threatened to deny Gudrun any contact with Dan if she broke up their marriage. He had agreed to bring up the child she had conceived with her lover as his own if she stayed with him.

No woman should ever be faced with the prospect of losing her child, Belle brooded. Gudrun had put her love for her son before her personal happiness, but because of that Belle had endured a miserable childhood, wondering why the man she believed was her father seemed to despise her. What a tangled mess it had been, she thought sadly. All brought about because her mother had married the wrong man. Gudrun's diary had revealed that she had known within a few months of the wedding that her marriage to John had been a mistake, but by then she had been pregnant with Dan and so had been trapped in a loveless relationship.

She would never make the same mistake, Belle vowed. She loved designing beautiful, romantic wedding gowns, but the idea of giving up her independence for a man held no appeal whatsoever. *Especially a man like Loukas Christakis.* The thought slid into her head as she glanced across the table and felt her stomach dip at the sight of his hard-boned features. He was the most breathtakingly handsome man she had ever laid eyes on, and she was sure he could be charming and charismatic when it suited him, but he was too forceful for her liking—too controlling—too much of a reminder of the man she had grown up believing to be her father.

She was wasting her time here. The rigid set of Loukas's square jaw told her that. Disappointment settled like a lead weight in the pit of her stomach and she suddenly felt desperate to escape his brooding presence. She drank the rest of her juice, set the glass down on the table and picked up her bag. 'All right, Mr Christakis. You win. If I take the next ferry back to Athens I may be able to catch a flight to London this evening.' She paused and then asked huskily, 'Can we make up an excuse for Larissa to explain why I'm not available to make her dress—a family emergency or something? I don't want her to think that I simply didn't turn up— which I'm sure *you* would allow her to believe,' she added accusingly.

Loukas did not reply immediately, and in the silence

that stretched between them his slate-grey gaze gave no clue to his thoughts. 'It matters to you what Larissa thinks?' he queried at last.

'Of course it does.' Belle gave him an impatient look. 'Your sister is a lovely person, and I'd hate her to think I'd let her down like her first designer did. I know you'll tell me it's none of my business, but I think you're wrong to interfere in her life—even if you have the best intentions for doing so,' she continued firmly when Loukas gave her a dark glare. 'There's a fine line between wanting to protect her and being too controlling, and you could find that Larissa will start to resent you for preventing her from making her own decisions.'

'You're right. My relationship with my sister is absolutely none of your business,' Loukas growled, irritated that her words had struck a nerve. He did not want to control Larissa; it was a ridiculous suggestion. He simply wanted to do what was best for her and take care of her—as he had promised his parents he would.

His mind turned to the past—to memories that still tugged on his soul. *You have to be a man now, son, and look after your mother and sister,'* his father had choked while the life had slipped from his body as fast as the blood had gushed from the gunshot wound to his stomach—courtesy of a couple of young punks high on crack. Loukas had been sixteen then, terrified of the responsibility that had been thrust upon him and ravaged with grief for his beloved Papa.

Two years later his mother had clutched his arm with a hand that was so thin he had been able to see every vein beneath her papery skin. Her cancer had been diagnosed too late for her to have a chance, and without health insurance or money to pay for the drugs that might have prolonged her life a little the end had come quickly. *'Take care of Larissa,'* had been the last words she had whispered. And standing by her bed, watching helplessly as she left the world, Loukas had given her his word.

How *dared* Belle Andersen criticise him? he thought furiously. She could have no idea what he had felt like at eighteen, knowing that he was totally responsible for his six-year-old sister. Life had been tough, and there had been many nights when he had been unable to sleep, scared that he wasn't strong enough to cope.

Of *course* he was over-protective of Lissa, he thought savagely. He'd had first-hand experience of how dangerous the world could be when he had witnessed his father's murder. But Belle's warning that Larissa might resent what she had termed his interference played on his mind. He recalled his sister's excitement when she had told him that Belle was coming to Aura to design her wedding dress.

Gamoto! he cursed silently. Maybe Belle had a point when she had said that Lissa should be free to make her own decisions. Maybe it was time he learned to take a step back and accept that his sister was no longer a child. Besides, what could go wrong? Belle would be on Aura, under his watchful gaze. She had said she was prepared to work night and day to complete Larissa's dress, and he would make sure she fulfilled her promise.

Once again his eyes were drawn to Belle's mouth, and he felt his body tighten with desire as he imagined plundering those soft pink lips. He could not deny his sizzling sexual attraction to her—and, more intriguingly, his instincts told him that she was as aware as he was of the white-hot chemistry between them.

Belle stood up from the table and held out her hand to Loukas. 'I'd like my phone back, please,' she said briskly. 'I need to ring the airport and see if I can change my return flight.'

He donned his sunglasses and got to his feet before he dropped her phone into her palm. His fingers only brushed against her hand for a few seconds but the contact of his skin against hers sent a tingling sensation up her arm. Belle jerked her hand back so quickly that she almost dropped her phone. She felt hot all over, every nerve ending quivering with her fierce awareness of him. Get a grip, she told herself impatiently, infuriated that he dominated her senses.

He was so tall. Now that they were both standing once more, Belle was struck anew by his size, his undoubted strength and his sheer, virile masculinity. Maybe it was a good thing she was going home, she thought shakily. She seemed incapable of controlling her body's response to Loukas—a fact that became shamefully obvious when she glanced down and saw the outline of her nipples jutting beneath the silky material of her jacket.

Face flaming, she crossed her arms defensively over her chest and began to scroll through the contacts in her phone's memory, searching for the number for Athens airport.

'Stop messing about and come with me now if you want a lift to Aura.'

She snapped her head up to find that Loukas was already holding the larger of her suitcases, and while she gaped at him he rounded the table, picked up her other case, and walked out of the bar.

'*Wait...*' His long stride had already taken him across the road. Belle teetered after him, cursing her vertiginous heels and the uneven cobbled surface of the quay. 'I don't understand.'

She finally caught up with him, and her heart lurched when he glanced down and subjected her to a cool stare. He was so incredibly good-looking, she thought helplessly. She was embarrassed by her reaction to him, but could not tear her eyes from the sculpted perfection of his hard-boned features.

'Do you mean I *can* make Larissa's dress?' She was confused by his sudden about-face, but why else would he have offered to take her to his island? 'Aren't you worried that I'll dupe your sister out of a fortune—like that Toula woman did—and then disappear, leaving her without a wedding dress?' she demanded bitterly, still fuming at his treatment of her.

'No, I'm not worried about that.' They had reached the edge of the quay and Loukas dropped her cases into his boat before turning to face her. 'I have every confidence that you will design the wedding gown of Larissa's dreams and make her very happy. Because if you don't—' his hard smile sent a shiver down Belle's spine '—you will answer to me.'

Belle finally lost control of her temper. Loukas Christakis wasn't just insulting and arrogant, he was a bully who clearly enjoyed bossing people around. But she'd been pushed around by John Townsend all her childhood—sometimes literally, she remembered grimly. She wasn't going to put up with it again from any man.

'Are you threatening me, Mr Christakis?' she demanded, placing her hands on her hips and wishing fervently that she was taller and did not have to tilt her head to meet his gaze.

'Merely warning you,' he said silkily. 'Disappoint me, and more importantly Larissa, and I promise you will find it impossible to gain financial backing for Wedding Belle anywhere in the world.'

She believed him. His wealth and his status as one of the most brilliant and ruthless businessmen of the decade gave him that kind of power. She had no doubt that he could destroy her little company as easily as he could crush an ant beneath his shoe.

'Well? Are you coming? I haven't got all day for you to make up your mind.'

She gave a start at the sound of his faintly mocking tone and realised that he had jumped into the boat and was holding out his hand to help her step on board. She would love to tell him to take a running jump, Belle thought viciously, preferably over the edge of a high cliff. But the stark truth was that she needed this job. If she could not start to pay back her business loan to the bank Wedding Belle would collapse without any help from Loukas.

In her high heels and pencil skirt there was no way she could climb into the boat without his help. Reluctantly she leaned forward to take his hand, and gave a startled cry when, having lost patience with her dithering, Loukas gripped her waist and swung her down from the quay.

The few seconds that he held her against him scrambled her brain, and the feel of his muscular torso and rock-hard thighs pressed so intimately close to her body was causing a coiling sensation deep in her pelvis. She snatched a breath when he set her down and gave him a fulminating glare, desperate to hide her awareness of him. 'Thank you,' she said icily, 'but I could have managed perfectly well, Mr Christakis—'

'Nonsense.' He cut her off mid-tirade. 'You're as wobbly as a newborn foal in those ridiculous shoes. And you'd better make it Loukas. My sister was keen that I should welcome you to Aura, and she'll expect us to be on first-name terms—Belle.'

Something about the way he said her name sent a little quiver through Belle, and his amused smile stole her breath. Already devastatingly sexy, the sudden upward curve of his sensual mouth caused her knees to sag, and she could feel her heart thundering as if she'd run a marathon.

'You'd better hold on to this before the wind whips it away.' Loukas lifted the elegant cream and black hat from Belle's head, and stiffened when pale gold hair unfurled and fell almost to her waist in a silken stream. He had been right about her being a blonde. In the sunlight her hair was the colour of platinum. It seemed unlikely that the shade was natural, but she was so tiny compared to his six-foot-four frame that her head only came halfway up his chest, and he could see no telltale sign of darker roots on her scalp.

The breeze blew a few fair strands across her face and, unable to stop himself, Loukas reached out and brushed the hair back from her cheek. Time was suspended. Belle's heart stopped beating as she stared into dark grey eyes that were no longer cold and hard as tensile steel, but glinting with a blatant sexual heat that evoked a shameful longing inside her for him to pull her into his arms and plunder her mouth with the savage passion she sensed he was capable of.

How could she be attracted to him when he was everything she hated? It was just a physical thing, she assured herself frantically—a chemical reaction that she had no control over. But somehow she would have to ignore her sexual attraction to Loukas if she was not going to spend the next week embarrassing herself by ogling him like a teenager with a severe crush.

The throb of the boat's engine seemed to reverberate through her, and she gripped the edge of her seat as he opened the throttle and sped out of the harbour, heading towards the small island of Aura—a green haven set amid the sparkling blue sea. Her hair whipping across her face, Belle glanced back at Kea, already far behind them. Sudden panic flooded through her and she felt an impending sense of unease that her life would never be the same again once she had set foot on Loukas Christakis's private domain.

CHAPTER THREE

'MOST of this side of Aura is covered in forest,' Loukas explained as they approached the island and Belle remarked on the distinctive dark green cypress trees that flanked the shoreline, standing like silent sentinels guarding the land.

There was no beach; the grey rocky cliffs sloped down to the sea, forming a natural harbour where a wooded jetty had been built. The sea appeared a brilliant turquoise colour from a distance, but as Loukas steered the boat into the shallows the water was so crystal-clear that Belle could see shoals of tiny fish darting like silver arrows. Fascinated by them, she leaned over and trailed her hand in the water, watching their scales glint and gleam in the sunlight.

'Aren't they beautiful?' she murmured, pushing her long hair over her shoulder.

Loukas fought the urge to run his fingers through the silky blonde strands, and concentrated on tying the boat securely to a post on the jetty. 'Speaking as the son of a fisherman, I don't think much of them; they'd only make a couple of mouthfuls,' he muttered.

'Oh, I wouldn't want to eat them. They're far too pretty.' Belle laughed, her resentment of Loukas's high-handed manner forgotten as she lifted her head and glanced about her, drinking in the view of the dense blue sky and sea and the rugged grey cliffs, which at close hand she could see were covered in a profusion of tiny pink flowers. 'What a heavenly place,' she said softly, the tension that had gripped her when they had left Kea seeping away.

Loukas could not look away from her. A man could drown in the depths of those incredible blue eyes, he brooded. And as for her smile! It lit up her gamine face and turned her classical features from beautiful to breathtaking.

He gave an impatient snort. Trouble! He'd known that was what Belle Andersen spelt. He should have followed his first instinct when he had seen her dainty figure teetering along the quay in her stiletto heels and turned the boat around. Instead he had brought her to his home—an honour he rarely conferred upon any woman, including his mistresses. Aura was his private haven, a place of peace and tranquillity where he could relax away from the pressures of work.

Right now he felt anything but relaxed, he thought derisively as he took Belle's hand to help her step onto the jetty, and inhaled the delicate floral fragrance of her perfume. His body had been aroused since he had lifted her into the boat at Kea and her breasts had brushed against his chest, and now, with his eyes drawn to the delightful sway of her bottom as she preceded him along the jetty, he could feel his erection straining uncomfortably beneath his jeans.

'*Theos,*' he growled beneath his breath. All he needed on top of running his business empire and arranging Larissa's wedding was an inconvenient attraction to a beautiful blonde who had the face of an angel but possessed a surprisingly sharp tongue.

A path ran from the jetty and climbed fairly steeply, disappearing around an outcrop of rock. 'It's only about a five-minute walk up to the house,' Loukas explained as he picked up both the suitcases, 'but the path is uneven in places.' He glanced down at Belle's new, shiny black patent stilettos that were probably her pride and joy, and grimaced. 'Do you think you'll manage? You might be better to change into more sensible footwear.'

Sensible! How she hated that word, Belle thought fiercely. It took her back in time to the countless arguments she'd had with John when she had been a teenager about her shoes, clothes, make-up. *I won't allow any daughter of mine to go around looking like a slut,* had been his favourite refrain, his face turning purple with temper, and his sergeant-major bark echoing through the house. He had known, of course—although back then Belle had not—that she was not his daughter. She had been a constant reminder of her mother's infidelity and John had taken his bitterness out on her. Heels higher than an inch had been banned, along with short skirts and tight jeans—all the modern things that her friends wore. *'You'll do as I say because I'm the adult and you're a child.'*

Rebelliousness had burned in Belle's heart every time John had bossed her around, and now the supercilious expression on Loukas's face evoked the same mutinous feeling.

'I always wear heels, and I can walk perfectly well in them,' she told him coolly. 'I'm sure I'll manage the path fine.' Head held high, she swung round, caught her heel on a tuft of grass at the edge of the path and stumbled, only saved from falling by Loukas's lightning reactions as he dropped the cases and grabbed her arm.

'Yes, I can see you're as sure-footed as a mountain goat,' he said dryly. 'Let's try again—carefully. And you'd better wear this.' He plonked her hat unceremoniously onto her head. 'The sun is at its hottest in the late afternoon, and with your fair skin you'll burn to the colour of a boiled lobster in no time.'

Without waiting to hear her reply he picked up the cases once more and strode ahead of her up the path, not turning his head to see if she was following.

Arrogant, pig-headed... Belle took a deep breath and marched behind him, her eyes focused on the ground to make sure she did not trip. On one hand Loukas made her feel five years old. But there had been nothing childlike about her response to him when he had lifted her into his boat, she thought ruefully, flushing as she remembered how her nipples had tingled when her breasts had brushed against his chest.

She sighed. Her unexpected attraction to Loukas was another complication to add to the fraught situation of trying to complete Larissa's wedding dress within a very tight deadline. She could only pray Larissa had spoken the truth when she'd said that her brother spent much of his time at his offices in Athens and often stayed at his apartment in the city, because she hoped to have as little to do with him as possible.

The path wound up to the top of the cliff, and at the summit Belle paused to take in the view. An endless expanse of shimmering blue sea was on one side, dotted with islands, the closest of which was Kea. To the other side of her the landscape of Aura was mainly grey rock, green vegetation, tall, slender cypress trees and dense olive groves, beneath which grew a carpet of brilliant red spring poppies.

'Do many people live on the island?' she asked Loukas, who had slowed his pace so that she could catch up with him. 'I see there is a village down in the valley.'

'Many years ago a small community, mainly fishermen, lived here. My father was born on Aura. But Kea has a bigger harbour, and gradually everyone moved away, leaving the island uninhabited until I bought it three years ago.'

'So no one lives in those houses?'

'My household staff and their families live in the village now. Many of the houses were in a bad state of repair, but I have a team of builders who are gradually restoring them. There is also a church where Larissa will be married.'

'I hope it's a big one,' Belle commented. 'Larissa told me that hundreds of guests have been invited to the wedding.'

Loukas grimaced. 'Yes, her fiancé has a huge extended family, most of whom Lissa has never met before. The church is tiny, and most of the guests will be seated in the square outside for the actual ceremony, but the reception will be at the villa, where there is much more room.'

Belle gave him a surprised look, wondering how big his villa was. 'Will there be room for so many guests to stay at your house?'

'*Theos*, no!' His horrified expression at the idea of his home being invaded by guests was almost comical, and made him seem a little more human, she mused, desperately trying to fight her awareness of him as she studied his superbly chiselled features. 'Most people will stay in Athens or on Kea. I've chartered a fleet of helicopters to ferry guests over to Aura, and some people will arrive by boat.'

'It sounds a logistical nightmare. Wouldn't it have been easier to have the wedding in Athens?'

Loukas shrugged. 'Probably. But Larissa wanted to be married here, and I'll move heaven and earth to give her the wedding she wants.'

Belle stared at him, startled by the sudden huskiness in his voice. There could be no doubt that Loukas adored his sister. The emotion blazing in his eyes was strangely humbling and made her wonder if she had misjudged him. Perhaps he wasn't as controlling as she had first thought? Certainly it seemed important to him that Larissa's wedding should be perfect.

They walked on in silence, the path wider now so that they were side by side. The views from the clifftop, of the sea and across the island, were stunning, and Belle was not surprised that Larissa wanted to hold her wedding in such a beautiful place. It was not Larissa Christakis who occupied her thoughts, however, but her brother.

'You said that your father was born here on Aura, but I take it that you were not?'

'No, the island had been abandoned long before then. I was born on Kea and spent my early childhood there. Larissa was also born there, but she has no memories of the place because we moved to America when she was very young.'

'Why did your family leave Greece?' Belle asked curiously.

'To make a living.' Loukas's mouth tightened as he

silently acknowledged the bitter irony of that statement. 'My father's fishing boat had been wrecked in a storm and he couldn't afford to buy a new one. But without a boat he couldn't fish and make money to feed his family. A distant cousin owned a grocery store in New York. Xenos arranged for us to move there so that my parents could run the shop, and when he died he left it to them.'

'It must have been a big change, moving from a small island to a city. I moved house dozens of times when I was growing up, because my stepfather was in the army and we lived wherever he was stationed.' She had hated being the new girl at school, always trying to fit in and make friends, Belle remembered. 'I would have found it even harder to settle in a new country.' She glanced towards the turquoise sea shimmering in the sunshine. 'Didn't you miss all this?'

'Every day. But I was young and better able to cope with the change.' His voice deepened. 'It broke my father's heart to leave Greece.'

'He must have been pleased when you bought Aura—his birthplace.'

Loukas hesitated for a moment, and then shrugged. The basic facts about his background could be found by anyone who chose to research him on the internet. 'He never knew. My father died eighteen months after we moved to the States, and my mother followed him to the grave two years later.'

His voice was so devoid of emotion that Belle shot him a startled glance. Despite the heat from the sun she shivered, sadness sweeping over her at the thought that Loukas's father had never come home, never seen again this beautiful place.

'I'm sorry. I didn't know—' She broke off abruptly. There was no reason why she should have known about the tragedy that had torn Loukas's family apart. She had met him less than an hour ago, they were strangers, so why did her heart ache for him? And why was she so sure that he concealed his pain behind his unfathomable grey gaze? Perhaps because she had learned to hide her own heartbreak at her mother's death and pretend that she wasn't hurting inside, she thought bleakly.

Another thought struck her. 'Larissa can't have been very old when your parents died. Who looked after her?'

Loukas had started walking again, and Belle fell in step beside him. 'I did. There was no one else. She barely remembers our father, and I have tried to be a father figure to her. But she missed having a mother. She still does—especially now, as she prepares for her wedding.' He gave a heavy sigh. 'You know how it is—there's a special bond between mothers and daughters.'

His words touched a raw nerve. A lump formed in Belle's throat and for a moment she could not speak. 'Yes,' she said at last in a low tone. 'I know how it is.' She stared at the horizon, the sharp line between the sea and the sky blurring as tears filled her eyes. She had shared a special bond with her mother—or at least she had believed she had. But in all those years that she was growing up, during all those mother-and-daughter shopping trips and girly chats, Gudrun had never revealed the truth about her father. The feeling of betrayal burned in her heart as fiercely as the pain of grief.

'Belle… Is something wrong?' Loukas suddenly realised that she had fallen behind and turned to find her standing looking out over the sea. Her face was half hidden beneath the brim of her hat, but he sensed her tangible vulnerability.

What the hell had got into him today? he wondered irritably. He was not one of the sensitive 'new-man' types so beloved by women's magazines; he was a hard-headed businessman who dealt in facts and figures, profit margins and takeover bids. Flights of imagination about the emotional well-being of any woman, let alone his sister's dress designer, whom he'd met for the first time an hour ago, were not in his nature.

He glanced at his watch and realised he was late to make an important call. He couldn't blame Belle if he'd missed out on the Tokyo deal, he conceded. But from now on he was determined to concentrate on business and not allow himself to be distracted by her.

'I was just admiring the view.' Belle blinked fiercely before she turned to Loukas. She could sense his impatience as he waited for her, and she pushed her dark thoughts to the back of her mind and walked towards him, determined to focus on the job she had come to Aura to do.

They continued along the path for a few more metres before it forked—one branch sloping down to a set of steps cut into the cliff, which led to a white sandy beach below, and the other stopping in front of a set of wrought-iron gates set in a high stone wall. Loukas pressed a button so that the gates swung smoothly open, and ushered Belle through.

'Welcome to the Villa Elena.'

'Oh…wow!' The stunning sight before her eyes jolted Belle from her painful memories. 'It's…spectacular,' she breathed, as she stared at the ultra-modern architecture of the white-walled villa with its many windows that must offer amazing views over the sea.

Loukas nodded. 'It's home,' he said simply.

Belle could have no idea how much those two words meant to him, he thought. Through all the years he had spent living in a grim tenement block in a rough neighbourhood in New York he had clung to his memories of his homeland, and had dreamed of one day owning a house overlooking the sapphire-blue waters of the Aegean.

Thanks to his quick brain, ruthlessness determination and years of relentless hard work, he had built his hugely successful company and achieved his dream. Aura was his bolthole, where he had created a home for him and Larissa.

It would have been his child's home too. *It should have been*. The familiar black bitterness filled his heart. He had bought the island when Sadie had told him she was pregnant, and commissioned an architect to design a luxurious villa for the woman he had loved and their baby.

But Sadie had never come here, and there had been no baby—she had made sure of that. His jaw hardened, his gut twisting at the memory of her betrayal. She had known how much he wanted his child, but she had refused to allow anything to stand in the way of her pursuit of stardom.

Larissa was the only person he had confided in, and it had been she who had begged him to stop anaesthetising his emotions with whisky. He would never forget how his little sister, whom he had cared for since their parents had died, had become the carer. Lissa had been there for him in his darkest days, when pain and anger had clawed at his insides. But soon she would leave the island and move to the house he had bought for her and Georgios in Athens. Loukas exhaled heavily. His little sister had grown up, and it was time to let her go, but he had not anticipated how hard he would find it.

He glanced briefly at Belle. 'Come on through,' he invited. 'My butler will know we're here and will serve drinks on the terrace.'

Butler! Of *course* he had a butler, Belle told herself as she followed him across the white marble patio. Loukas was a billionaire and he probably had dozens of staff to run around him.

She realised that they had entered the villa grounds by a side gate. The house was to the right of her, while on her left they skirted a large circular Jacuzzi and continued on towards an infinity pool that gave the illusion of spilling over the edge of the cliff into the sea below. In the bright sunshine everything seemed to throb with an intensity of colour: the gleaming white walls of the villa, the aquamarine of the pool and the sea, and the vibrant oranges, reds and yellows of the flowers set amidst the lush greenery of the landscaped garden. It was paradise, Belle thought, feeling almost dizzy from the beauty of her surroundings.

As they walked towards the terrace and stepped into the shade of the white awning fluttering gently in the breeze, a man walked out of the house to meet them.

'This is Chip,' Loukas introduced the man. Short and stocky, with a shock of red hair and wearing brightly coloured Bermuda shorts, Chip was not what Belle had imagined a butler to be. His broad grin told her he knew what she was thinking.

'How ya doin?' he greeted her in a strong American drawl.

'As you can't fail to notice, Chip has a penchant for loud shorts,' Loukas said dryly. 'It's the reason I always wear sunglasses. But he's worked for me for years and so I have to forgive him for his terrible taste in clothes.'

The butler chuckled. There was clearly a strong friendship between the two men that went deeper than simply employer and employee, Belle thought. As if he had read her mind Loukas continued, 'Chip and I spent our teenage years living in the South Bronx. Back then there was a lot of trouble between gangs—a lot of violence on the streets. We used to watch each other's backs.' He did not elaborate, but Belle sensed from the look that passed between the two men that they had experienced incidences of street violence, and had relied on each other perhaps for their very survival.

'It's nice to meet you, Chip,' she murmured, giving him a smile. 'Actually, I like your shorts.'

'Thank you, Ms Andersen. It's nice to meet someone else with good taste.' He winked at her as he set the tray down on the table, and indicated the teapot. 'Larissa told me you like to drink tea. I hope Earl Grey is okay for you?'

'Oh, yes—lovely.' Belle took the china cup and saucer Chip handed her and sipped the delicately flavoured tea with pleasure. 'Heavenly.'

'Drinking tea is an English custom I'll never understand,' Loukas said with a grimace, taking the glass of cold beer his butler offered him. 'Can you take Belle's cases up to her room, Chip?'

Once the butler had disappeared into the house Belle's intense awareness of Loukas returned with a vengeance.

She finished her tea and put the cup back on the saucer with a slightly unsteady hand. 'I'm really looking forward to seeing Larissa,' she murmured, looking towards the house in the hope that the Greek girl would soon appear.

'I'm afraid you'll have to wait until tomorrow.' Loukas savoured his last mouthful of beer and set his glass back on the tray. 'Lissa flew to Athens on my helicopter a couple of hours ago. Her fiancé's father has been rushed into hospital, and she wanted to be with Georgios as the family wait for news on Constantine's condition.'

Taken aback by this unexpected news, Belle stared at him. 'I'm sorry to hear that. Is Georgios's father very ill?'

'He has a heart condition and is due to have major surgery next month. When Larissa was let down by her first designer she suggested moving the wedding forward a few weeks, which would have meant it was after Constantine's operation, to give enough time for her dress to be made. But I pushed for her to stick to the original date,' Loukas admitted. 'The operation is high risk, and if things were to go wrong—well, let's just say I believed it prudent to have the wedding before Constantine's surgery. Not that I let Larissa know of my concerns that Georgios's father might not pull through,' he added. 'She's very fond of him, and she and Georgios would be devastated if he did not see them marry.'

Once again Belle heard the fierce protectiveness Loukas felt for his sister in his voice. It sounded as though his insistence that the wedding should take place in a month's time, as originally planned, was not because it suited his work schedule, but because he was concerned for Larissa's future father-in-law. Maybe he wasn't as much of a control freak as she had first thought?

She frowned as another thought occurred to her. 'If you knew Larissa wasn't here, why didn't you say so when we were on Kea? Why did you bring me to Aura?' Why did she feel so unsettled by the realisation that she was alone with Loukas on his island? They were not completely alone, she reminded herself. Chip was here, and no doubt a team of staff must be needed to run the huge villa. There was no reason for her heart-rate to quicken. But Loukas had removed his sunglasses and his narrowed gaze was focused on her mouth. Instinctively she wet her dry lips with the tip of her tongue and saw him stiffen, the expression in his eyes becoming preda-tory, hungry. Her heart gave a jolt.

'I could have stayed on Kea and checked into a hotel until Larissa returned to Aura,' she said a little desperately.

He shrugged. 'I assumed you would want to see where the wedding is to be held. Larissa explained that you take the venue into consideration when design-ing the dress. She's coming back tomorrow morning. I thought you might as well unpack and settle in before she arrives.'

What was it about this man and his determination to control other people's lives? 'You should have told me,' Belle said stiffly. 'I prefer to make my own decisions.'

'It's no big deal, is it?' Loukas wondered why Belle seemed so edgy. She was looking at him suspiciously and he felt his irritation grow. Did she think he was going to jump on her like some testosterone-fuelled youth? Hell, he wasn't the only one of them to feel the magnetic pull of sexual attraction. He had noticed the way she kept darting him little glances, the way she touched her tongue to her lips whenever he looked at her.

'You seem to be worried about something, Belle,' he said softly, feeling a flare of satisfaction when he strolled towards her and she immediately took a step backwards. Definitely edgy—and flustered. He wondered if she wanted him to kiss her as badly as he wanted to.

'I'm not worried about anything,' she denied sharply, carefully avoiding his gaze. 'What should I be worried about?'

The fact that he was sorely tempted to pull her into his arms, lower his head and ravage her soft, pink, moist lips, he thought self-derisively. He was so close to her now that he could see his reflection in her dark pupils. He watched them dilate and heard her breathing quicken. Oh, yes, she was definitely flustered. She hooked a strand of long blonde hair behind her ear and he was suddenly struck by how young she looked. His thoughts cannoned into one another in his head and arrived at the same conclusion: she was a complication he could do without.

'Nothing,' he said abruptly, jerking away from her. 'You're absolutely safe on Aura. There's no crime here— not even any cars to cause accidents.' He was waffling— a phenomenon he'd never experienced before—and his irritation with himself increased. 'Come with me and I'll show you to your room.' He walked briskly across the terrace. 'I'll be working from my office here at the villa for the rest of the day, but if you need anything just use the house phone to call Maria. She's my cook and housekeeper, and Chip's wife,' he explained when

Belle gave him an enquiring glance. 'Other members of staff come in from the village every day to help run the house, but I value my privacy and none of my staff live at the Villa Elena.'

He strode into the house, and Belle forced herself to follow him on legs that felt decidedly unsteady. That was the second time in the space of the afternoon that she had thought Loukas was about to kiss her, she thought shakily. He had stood so close to her that her skin had tingled with anticipation that he would take her in his arms and draw her against his hard body. She had been certain that he was about to lower his head and slant his mouth over hers, and she had been waiting for his kiss, longing to feel the demanding pressure of his lips, she admitted, flushing when she recalled how she had swayed towards him.

What had got into her? she asked herself angrily. She had come to Aura to work on probably the most important commission of her career and she could *not* allow herself to be distracted by her shockingly fierce sexual attraction to Loukas. It was so unlike her. She was usually so calm and controlled, but for some reason he decimated her composure.

Much of the ground floor of the Villa Elena was open-plan, creating a huge, airy living space broken up by furniture arranged in groups: pale leather sofas and chairs, a dining area with a long glass table, a corner dominated by a state-of-the-art plasma TV. It was bright and modern, minimalist chic, yet somehow it still managed to be homely and comfortable—an effect that Belle knew only the best and most expensive interior designers were capable of producing.

The room she had been allocated was at the end of a

long hallway on the second floor. Her heart leapt with pleasure when Loukas threw open the door to reveal a charming bedroom overlooking a grove of lemon trees, beyond which she could glimpse the sea.

'I'll send one of the maids up to help you unpack. From the size of your suitcase you must have brought enough clothes for a year,' he commented, glancing at the two cases on the bed.

'The bigger case contains all my material samples and design ideas,' Belle told him, opening the lid to reveal layers of silks and satins in pure white, ivory and pastel pink. 'I think Larissa will love this silk organza.' She touched the material almost reverently. 'Although she may want something heavier, like this satin—perhaps embellished with tiny crystals or pearls. I guess I'll just have to be patient and wait until Larissa gets here,' she murmured, when Loukas gave her a look that said she might as well be speaking in a foreign language for all the sense she was making to him.

He picked up her portfolio and flicked through the pages, but he made no comment and his hard features gave no clue to his opinion of her work.

Her enthusiasm was undeniable, Loukas brooded as he dragged his gaze from Belle's animated face and stared down at the portfolio. He was no expert, but he could see instantly that she was a talented designer. The photographs of gowns from her collection were stunning, and he understood now why Larissa was so keen for Belle to make her dress.

He glanced at her, his eyes drawn to her against his will, and felt something kick in his gut when she pushed her hair over her shoulder. She used her whole body when she spoke, tilting her head and moving her arms and hands with the grace of a ballerina.

He tensed at the thought and slammed a mental door shut on memories he refused to dwell on—memories of another woman who had moved with the instinctive grace of a dancer. He would not waste a second of his life thinking about Sadie. Even the memory of her name was offensive to him.

The room suddenly seemed claustrophobic—or was it his fascination with the dainty blonde he'd brought to Aura that was bothering him? He strode over to the door. 'I have to get back to work. Please make yourself at home at the villa, Belle,' he said coolly. 'Would you like Maria to bring you another pot of tea?'

Desperate to distract herself from the fact that Loukas's sun-bleached jeans were stretched taut over his muscular thighs, Belle had wandered over to the window. 'Actually, I think I'll go for a walk and find the church.'

She turned to find Loukas frowning. 'That's not a sensible idea. I've already explained that the sun is at its hottest in the late afternoon,' he said, sounding impatient. 'I suggest you relax for the rest of the day. You can swim in the pool if you want,' he added, stepping into the hall and shutting the door without giving Belle the chance to respond.

Irritating man, she fumed. Anyone would think she was five years old. His use of the word *sensible* was like a red rag to a bull. She was aware that she wasn't used to the heat, but all she'd suggested was a short stroll—not to run a marathon.

Inside her head she heard John shouting at her. *'Don't*

argue with me. Do as I say. It's time you learned to obey orders, my girl.'

Sergeant-Major John Townsend had treated his family in the same way that he'd treated the soldiers under his command and had expected obedience at all times—especially from Belle. But she had never been John's girl, and since she had learned the truth she was determined to stand up for herself after a lifetime of having her self-confidence stripped from her. She was Loukas Christakis's guest on his private island, but she would *not* stand for him bossing her around, she vowed fiercely.

CHAPTER FOUR

MUTTERING a curse beneath his breath, Loukas forced his gaze back to his computer screen and tried to ignore the sight of Belle, wearing a tiny green and gold bikini, stretched out on a sun lounger just outside his study window. The Japanese deal was almost secured; all he needed to do was finish checking through the final details. But to his intense annoyance he could not concentrate.

Out of the corner of his eye he could see the brilliant blue infinity pool sparkling invitingly in the bright sunshine. Usually he found the view from his study relaxing, but right now he felt tense and unable to focus on the latest deal for Christakis Holdings. He skimmed down the page of the document on his screen and realised he had not taken in any of the information.

Outside the window Belle sat up and ran her fingers through her long blonde hair. Loukas gave up trying to work and watched her stand up and walk to the edge of the pool. She was petite, but perfectly in proportion, he noted, his gaze lingering on her slender thighs before moving up to her tiny waist and the surprisingly full breasts that were barely covered by the triangles of her bikini top.

Desire jackknifed inside him, startling him with its ferocity. What was it about Belle Andersen that turned him on so hard? he wondered impatiently, shifting in his seat in an attempt to alleviate the discomfort of his arousal straining beneath his jeans. She was beautiful, but no more so than hundreds of other women he had met over the years. He could not understand why he was so attracted to her, but sexual chemistry defied logical explanation, he realised as he jerked to his feet and strode out of the study.

The heat of the sun on her back was soporific. Belle wriggled her shoulders and gave a contented sigh. This was bliss, she thought sleepily. When she had first come down to the pool she had felt guilty—after all, she had come to Aura to work, not laze around in the sun. She'd recalled Dan's teasing comments when she had announced that she would be spending a week in Greece. But until Larissa arrived she could not begin to design her wedding dress. There had seemed no point in sitting in her bedroom for the rest of the day, and so she had changed into her new bikini which, to her dismay, was rather more revealing than she'd realised when she had bought it, gathered up her towel and book, and made her way down to the terrace.

Thankfully she had seen no sign of Loukas. Hopefully he would remain in his study for the rest of the day. Even though she was half asleep her muscles tensed when she pictured his arrogantly handsome features. Liquid heat flooded through every part of her body and pooled low in her pelvis. If she had known that Larissa's brother was so drop-dead sexy she might have had second thoughts about coming to Aura, she acknowledged ruefully.

The air was so still and quiet; only the occasional call of a cicada disturbed the silence. Belle's eyelashes drifted down and her muscles relaxed once more as sleep washed over her.

'Have you no common sense?' A voice—deep, accented and laced with impatience—roused her, and she opened her eyes to find Loukas hunkered down beside her, his dark brows drawn into a frown. 'Your fair skin will burn to a crisp if you lie out for much longer,' he said tersely, ignoring her gasp as he poured something cold between her shoulderblades. 'You should have applied sunscreen before you fell asleep,' he told her, when Belle turned her head and gave him a startled look.

'I did,' she defended herself breathlessly, struggling to drag air into her lungs while Loukas was smoothing the cream onto her shoulders. There was nothing remotely intimate about his actions, she told herself frantically. The feel of his strong fingers stroking briskly across her skin had no right to feel this good.

'Yes, but that was before you swam in the pool. You should have put more on when you got out of the water.' The memory of watching her anointing her half-naked body with suncream when she had first stepped out onto the terrace caused Loukas to harden, and he inhaled sharply, glad that she was lying on her front and hopefully could not see the evidence of his arousal.

He was so damned bossy, Belle thought angrily. It was on the tip of her tongue to tell him she could look after herself and didn't need any help from him, but the glide of his fingertips across her shoulderblades was strangely relaxing, and seemed to be unlocking all the knots of tension. She swallowed when he smoothed more cream onto her back, and found herself wishing that he would continue to slide his hands all the way down her spine. Thank heavens she was lying face down, so he could not see that her nipples had hardened. Her breasts felt heavy, and she was conscious of a hot, aching sensation between her thighs as her treacherous mind imagined him pulling her bikini pants down and stroking his hand over her bare bottom.

What had got into her? Her face burned with embarrassment and she felt a mixture of relief and sharp disappointment when he abruptly stood up.

'That should do,' he growled, stepping away from her. Something in his voice caused her to dart him a quick glance, and another wave of heat swept through her veins when her eyes met his and she saw undisguised feral hunger gleaming in his steel-grey gaze. For a few seconds the air seemed to tremble with a tangible tension, and only when he turned away and dived into the pool did Belle release her breath.

She sat up and reached for the pretty sarong that matched her bikini, hastily wrapping it around her body. Loukas was powering up and down the pool in a fast front crawl. Belle was tempted to hurry back into the house and escape from him before she made a complete fool of herself, but would it look too obvious that she was running away from him? While she was silently debating what to do he climbed up the steps out of the pool, water streaming from him, and she found herself rooted to her lounger.

Fully dressed, he was impossibly handsome, but in a pair of wet, black swim-shorts that clung to his powerful thigh muscles he was devastating. His skin gleamed like polished bronze and water droplets glistened on the whorls of dark hair that covered his chest and arrowed down over his flat abdomen. Belle's eyes strayed lower, but the sight of a distinct bulge beneath his shorts caused her to jerk her head upright, her face flaming.

Her heart pounded when he dragged a sun lounger closer to hers and sat down so that he was facing her. He lifted a hand to rake his wet hair back from his brow, and she hastily tore her eyes from his sculpted features, so acutely conscious of him that her skin prickled.

'So, Belle, tell me about yourself.' The request sounded more like an order than an invitation. 'Larissa told me you work mainly from a studio in west London?'

'Yes, Wedding Belle is based in Putney. My studio is in an old warehouse by the Thames, not far from where I live.'

'Do you own a house by the river?'

'I wish! Riverside properties are hugely expensive,' Belle told him ruefully. 'Dan and I rent an old houseboat.'

'Dan Townsend is your brother—the photographer—is that right?' Loukas recalled her telling him that she and her brother had different surnames. 'Do just the two of you live on the boat?'

Belle nodded, thinking of the cramped home she shared with Dan. 'Believe me, there's no room to swing a cat, let alone for anyone else to live on board.'

Why on earth was he pleased that she did not live with a boyfriend? It did not matter to him where Belle lived, or who she lived with, Loukas reminded himself. But he could not stop looking at her, and couldn't help imagining how soft her lips would feel beneath his. His body stirred. Clearly ten laps of the pool had not been enough to bring his libido under control, he thought grimly.

'What made you decide to be a fashion designer?' he queried—not because he cared about her choice of career, but because he needed to keep the conversation flowing so that he did not give in to the urge to push her onto her back on the sun lounger and settle his aroused body between her slender thighs.

'Art was the only subject I was any good at when I was at school,' Belle admitted. 'I was a terrible day-dreamer, but I loved drawing, and from a young age I used to make clothes for my dolls. Being a fashion designer was the only thing I felt I might have a chance of succeeding at.'

She bit her lip, remembering how she had struggled with subjects like math and science. John's biting sarcasm every time he read out her end of term reports had added to her belief that she was a failure, but her mother had encouraged her talent, and had supported her decision to go to art college.

'When I graduated, I worked briefly for a big wedding company. I found that I loved designing wedding dresses, but many of my ideas were deemed too unconventional by the head of the company, and so I decided to set up my own business.'

She fell silent, her eyes drawn to Loukas, and her heart lurched when she discovered that he was watching her intently. His gaze narrowed and focused on her mouth. His kiss would be no gentle seduction. The thought pushed into her head and sent a little shiver of reaction down her spine. Unconsciously she leaned towards him and moistened her bottom lip with the tip of her tongue, enslaved by his virile magnetism and a mystical alchemy she had no control over.

'Inconvenient, isn't it?' Loukas drawled softly. The

sound of his voice snapped her to her senses and she jerked back from him, blushing fiercely.

'What?'

'The sexual attraction between us,' he said calmly.

The matter-of-fact tone with which he delivered the statement shook Belle as much as his words. She gaped at him, but even as her mind fiercely rejected his outrageous statement she felt a tightening sensation deep in her pelvis.

'The…there isn't anything between us,' she faltered, desperately denying the suggestion. 'I don't…'

He cut her off by placing a finger across her lips, his steel-grey eyes trapping her gaze. 'There is, and you feel it—just as I do. The sexual chemistry was white-hot from the minute we laid eyes on each other,' he stated with supreme self-assurance.

Loukas could no longer deny his rampant desire for Belle. He had given up trying to rationalise why he wanted her so badly. Some things were beyond explanation or reasoning. Some things were purely instinctive. And his instincts now were demanding that he should taste her soft, moist lips.

This time he was going to kiss her. Belle read the message in Loukas's eyes and her heart stopped beating—suspended, as time was suspended, as he leaned forward and slowly lowered his head.

It was madness. She had only met him a few hours ago, her brain pointed out. She was here to work for his sister. Loukas had been opposed to her making Larissa's wedding dress. Maybe he was playing a game with her, trying to distract her so that he could then accuse her of not being focused on the job he had brought her to Aura to do?

Her mind whirled. The sensible part of her told her to push him away. But she could feel the warmth that emanated from his body, her senses were seduced by the musky scent of his cologne, and she was trapped by a desperate yearning to feel his mouth on hers. Her heart slammed against her ribs as his mouth hovered above hers and she felt his warm breath whisper against her lips.

The *thwump-thwump* of helicopter rotorblades above their heads shattered the silence and jerked Loukas to his senses. 'That'll be Larissa,' he said tersely. And just in time, he thought grimly. What the hell was he playing at? He had brought Belle to Aura to design his sister's wedding dress, not to seduce her into his bed. 'She phoned earlier to say she was on her way back to Aura.'

Belle snatched oxygen into her lungs, stunned that Loukas had not kissed her after all, and mortified by how much she had wanted him to. 'I hope she didn't rush back on my account,' she muttered, jumping to her feet at the same moment that he stood up, and catching her breath when their bodies touched briefly.

She sprang away from him as if the fleeting contact had burned her. The air seemed to vibrate with tension. This was *crazy*, taunted a little voice inside her. How could she be so drawn to a man she had only met that day? How could she wish that he would push her down onto the sun lounger and strip off her bikini to expose her naked body to his hungry gaze? She simply didn't do things like that. Her only sexual encounter had been with a fellow art student whom she had dated briefly at university. It had been a fumbling, unsatisfactory experience after they'd both had too much to drink, and she had never felt any desire to repeat the experience with him or anyone else—until now.

She cleared her throat and forced herself to speak. 'Do you know how her fiancé's father is?'

'I understand that Constantine is stable. Lissa would have remained at the hospital with Georgios if she was at all worried.'

Loukas needed to get away from Belle and clear his head. He felt out of control when he was around her, and he hated the feeling. Clearly the past month that he'd gone without sex was a month too long, he thought sardonically. There were several women in Athens he could call—casual relationships, with no expectations on either side. But although his mistresses were sophisticated and beautiful, none of them excited him as much as the elfin blonde who was watching him with a hungry expression in her eyes that made him wish his sister had remained in Athens for a few more hours.

'I suggest you go and get some clothes on,' he said over his shoulder as he strode towards the house. 'I'm sure Larissa will be eager to discuss your ideas for her dress.'

Five minutes after Belle had returned to her room there was a knock on her door and Larissa Christakis burst in.

'Belle! I'm so sorry I wasn't here when you arrived. It's been a mad day, with Georgios's father being rushed into hospital.' The young Greek woman gave Belle an apologetic smile. 'Luckily, Loukas offered to collect you from Kea. I hope he's been looking after you?'

Fortunately Belle was spared having to make a response when Larissa spied the suitcase of sample materials on the bed. 'As you can see, I'm all ready to get started on designing your dress,' she murmured.

'I can't wait.' Larissa could not hide her excitement. Tall and slender, she had a dream figure to design for, and her light olive complexion and mass of black curls would suit a pure white dress, Belle mused. 'But Loukas says you are tired after travelling today, and that we should wait until tomorrow to start work.'

Loukas wasn't under pressure to make three dresses in five weeks. Belle stifled her irritation and queried lightly, 'Does everyone always do everything Loukas says?'

'Oh, yes,' Larissa replied cheerfully. 'Loukas takes charge of everything. I don't know what I'd do without him. He's been brilliant organising the wedding.' She smiled softly. 'My brother is the best person in the world—apart from Georgios, of course. Our parents died when I was a kid, and Loukas brought me up. He made a lot of sacrifices so that he could take care of me.' Her smile became rueful. 'I'm just glad that when he needed help a few years ago I was able to care for him.'

'Why? What happened?' Belle asked curiously. 'Was he ill?' She couldn't imagine why a strong, powerful man like Loukas would need to be cared for.

Larissa looked awkward, as if regretting that she had spoken. 'There was a woman who broke his heart. It took him a long time to get over her, and for a while he turned to drink to dull the pain she caused him.'

Shock jolted through Belle. It was almost impossible to think of arrogant, self-assured Loukas being heart-broken. 'Did he love her?' she asked, unable to disguise her curiosity.

Larissa nodded sombrely. 'Yes, he wanted to marry her.' She shook her head as if to clear her thoughts. 'But, as I said, it was a few years ago. Dinner is at eight,' she went on, clearly determined to change the subject. 'Georgios's father's condition has stabilised, so Georgios and his sisters, Cassia and Acantha, who are to be my bridesmaids, have come to Aura to meet you.'

'Great.' Belle forced herself to concentrate on the reason she had come to Aura. 'I'm looking forward to discussing my ideas for your dress and showing you the material samples.'

'Well, if you're sure you want to start now, there's an empty room up on the top floor that Loukas says we can use.'

'What a fantastic view,' Belle commented ten minutes later as she crossed the large room Larissa had ushered her into and stared out of the window at the panoramic view of the sea.

'It's wonderful from this high up, isn't it? The view from the roof terrace is even better,' Larissa told her. 'You reach it by the spiral staircase we passed in the hall. Loukas says that at night it feels as though you could reach up and touch the stars.'

She opened the suitcase Belle had carried up and lifted out a swatch of ivory silk tulle. 'Oh, this is beautiful. I must go and call Cassia and Acantha—they're almost as excited as I am.'

The following hours flew past, as Belle discussed with Larissa and her bridesmaids numerous choices of material for their dresses, and began to sketch some ideas.

'Help—we're eating in twenty minutes,' Larissa suddenly said, glancing at her watch. 'I'd better go and change. Loukas hates people to wear jeans to dinner.'

Belle had been so absorbed in her ideas for the dresses that she had almost forgotten about him, but now an image of his handsome face flooded her mind, a memory of that near kiss by the pool, and she was annoyed to feel her heart flip at the prospect of seeing him again.

Back in her room, she changed into a silvery grey silk halter-neck dress which was one of her own designs. The only reason she had decided to wear it was to prove to Loukas that she was a skilled designer, she assured herself—not because she looked good in it. She was proud of her work, and of this dress in particular. Its deceptively simple lines flattered her slender figure and she loved the fluidity of the material, the way it gently swished around her ankles when she walked.

There was no time to do anything fancy with her hair, so she left it loose, fixed tiny diamond stud earrings to her lobes and a delicate silver chain around her neck, sprayed her pulse-points with perfume, and took a deep breath before stepping out of her room.

CHAPTER FIVE

'I LOVE your dress,' Larissa said admiringly, when Belle crossed the huge open-plan living room to the dining area. The long glass table had been decorated with white roses and candles which flickered in the soft breeze drifting in through the open French doors, while outside the terrace was lit by lamps which dappled the pool with their shimmering reflection.

The setting was beautiful and relaxing, but Belle had been fiercely conscious of Loukas's enigmatic gaze as he had watched her approach, and her heart-rate had quickened with every step that had brought her closer to him.

'Is it one of your own creations?' Larissa's voice helped distract her from her intense awareness of him, and when she nodded in affirmation the Greek girl gave a triumphant smile. 'Didn't I tell you Belle is a brilliant designer?' she demanded of her brother.

'Indeed you did,' Loukas drawled. His bland tone gave away nothing of his private thoughts. It was a pity his sister had not warned him that Belle was a gorgeous blonde sex-kitten who would have a profound effect on his libido, he thought sardonically. She looked stunning in her silvery dress—but she would look good in anything she wore, and even better wearing nothing at all, taunted a little voice in his head. Desire corkscrewed in his gut, and he was grateful for Larissa's bright chatter to cover his silence while he fought to bring his hormones under control.

'Belle, this is Georgios.'

Belle smiled at the young man at Larissa's side. 'I'm pleased to meet you. I'm sorry to hear of your father's health problems.'

'Thank you. The heart specialist is talking about bringing the date of his operation forward. It is a worrying time for all of us, especially my mother, but my father is insistent that we should continue with the wedding arrangements as planned.'

They took their places at the table, and Belle quickly slid into the seat furthest away from Loukas. Chip, resplendent in a dark suit, winked at her as he served the first course. 'Thought I'd better change out of my Bermudas, as the boss has guests for dinner,' he said conspiratorially.

Beneath Chip's gruff exterior it was evident that he felt a deep affection for 'the boss,' Belle noted, recalling how Loukas had said they had been friends since they were teenagers living in a rough part of New York. She darted a glance along the table and stiffened when her eyes clashed with Loukas's brooding stare. Something about the way he was looking at her caused her heart to race. Her face grew warm and she wanted to drag her gaze from him, but she was trapped by the sultry gleam in grey eyes that were no longer cold and hard, but blazing with sensual heat.

Her breath seemed to be trapped in her lungs and her eyes widened with a mixture of panic and fierce sexual awareness. Her mind flew back to those moments by the pool when he had smoothed suncream onto her shoulders. She had denied that she was attracted to him, but she knew she had been lying—and from the predatory expression on Loukas's face, he knew it too.

This was crazy, she thought desperately, as she finally summoned the willpower to break free from his magnetic hold and stared down at the warm goat's cheese salad starter in front of her. Never in her life had she felt so intensely aware of a man.

Having witnessed her mother's unhappy marriage to John Townsend, she had always been wary of relationships, and more importantly of making a mistake as Gudrun had done. She had never experienced an overwhelming attraction such as she felt for Loukas, and her every instinct warned her to fight it—but that was easier said than done, she thought ruefully, when her eyes were once more drawn to his sculpted profile and molten heat flooded through her.

'So, Belle, what made you decide to specialise in designing wedding dresses?' Georgios's voice caused her to jerk her gaze guiltily from Loukas. 'Are you a romantic at heart?'

About to deny it, Belle looked across the table and hesitated when she saw the adoring glance that passed between Larissa and her fiancé.

'I think it is a wonderful thing if two people fall in love and feel certain that they are right for each other and want to spend their lives together,' she said slowly. 'Weddings are joyful occasions and I love the fact that I help to make the day special by designing the bride's dress.'

But all too often that feeling of certainty turned out

to be a mistake, she thought to herself. Her mother's marriage to John had been a disaster. How could anyone really be sure they would be happy with another person for ever? she wondered. As for bringing children into a relationship—it seemed such an enormous concept. You would have to have absolute faith in a person before you had a child with them. She knew from her own difficult childhood that if the parents' relationship failed, their child was likely to suffer the consequences.

She suddenly realised that everyone around the table was waiting for her to continue. 'To be honest I can't afford to have my head full of romantic ideals when I'm running my own business,' she explained. 'I'm determined to make Wedding Belle a success, so my dresses are romantic, but I have to be practical and focused.'

'You would describe yourself as a hard-headed career woman, then, would you?'

Belle was puzzled by the hard edge to Loukas's tone and infuriated by the mockery in his smile. She had pleaded with him to give her the chance to design Larissa's dress, but if he believed he could walk all over her he'd better think again. 'Yes,' she replied coolly. 'As a businessman yourself, I'm sure you appreciate why I give single-minded dedication to my company.'

His dark brows arched quizzically. 'As your career is so important to you, does that mean you won't be designing your own wedding dress any time soon?'

Now there was something else in his hard-as-flint gaze—a gleam that sent a quiver down her spine. 'I have no plans in that direction,' she informed him crisply, relief surging through her when Cassia reopened the debate that had begun earlier about the colour of the bridesmaids' dresses.

'How long do you think it will take you to complete the designs for Larissa's wedding gown?' Loukas enquired at the end of the meal.

Belle savoured her last spoonful of decadently rich chocolate mousse before turning her head towards him, and once again her heart gave an annoying little flip. She wondered if he always dressed formally for dinner. He looked breathtakingly sexy in his black tuxedo and white silk shirt, and the piercing intensity of his stare decimated her fragile composure.

Somehow she forced a breezy smile. 'We made a start before dinner. I should easily have the final sketches completed by the end of the week, and once Larissa has chosen the materials she wants I can place the order with my suppliers. Then I'll go back to my studio to begin making the dresses.'

Loukas frowned. 'Does that mean that Larissa and her bridesmaids will have to travel to London for fittings?'

'Well, yes—but that will only be necessary two or at the most three times.' Belle wondered where this conversation was leading.

'Three trips to England over the next five weeks could be difficult when the wedding is so close and there are so many other arrangements to be made—don't you agree, Lissa?' Loukas glanced at his sister. 'And I'm sure you would prefer to remain in Greece now that Constantine's health is a concern.'

Larissa nodded slowly. 'Of course it would make life easier if I didn't have to fit in trips to London.' She voiced the question on the tip of Belle's own tongue. 'But what do you suggest? Belle can't move her studio to Greece.'

'Why not?'

It was Belle's turn to frown. 'It would be impossible. 'I have all the equipment I need at my studio—cutting tables, tailor's dummies, sewing machines.'

'But if I could provide you with everything you require, why couldn't you stay here on Aura to make the dresses?' Loukas asked smoothly. 'The room you were using earlier is a suitable size for a workroom, isn't it?

'Well—yes, but...' Belle was flummoxed by Loukas's suggestion. 'It would be an unnecessary expense for you to buy or even hire everything. A good sewing machine can cost several thousand pounds. Because Wedding Belle is only a small company I do a lot of the actual sewing myself, but I also employ two seamstresses, and I'm sure neither Doreen or Joan would be prepared to leave their families and come to Aura.'

He shrugged. 'The cost is immaterial. And if necessary I'm sure I could find a seamstress in Athens to help out. All I care about is ensuring that the run-up to the wedding is as stress-free as possible for Larissa, and one way to do that is for you make her dress here on Aura.'

Where he could keep a check on her progress, Belle thought furiously. He hadn't said the words out loud, but she knew what he was thinking and anger surged through her. Here again was another example of how Loukas liked to be in total control. But how could she argue with his desire to help his sister? She hadn't missed the hopeful look on Larissa's face when Loukas had made his suggestion.

'You seem to forget that I have a business to run in London,' she murmured, trying to keep her tone light for Larissa's benefit.

'Do you have many other commissions at present?' Loukas gave her a bland smile, but beneath his polite tone she detected a steely determination to have his own way. 'Perhaps one of your staff could be left in charge of your company while you stay here? There will, of course, be a financial reward for your co-operation. And let's not forget the valuable media exposure Wedding Belle will gain from this commission.'

Belle knew she was beaten, and her fears were confirmed when Larissa said excitedly, 'Oh, Belle, it would be wonderful if you could stay. It will mean I can be involved with my dress at every stage. And you'll be an honoured guest at the wedding.'

How on earth could she disappoint Larissa, who had already suffered one disappointment when the first designer she had commissioned had let her down, and who was now clearly worried about her fiancé's father? 'I suppose it's possible,' she said slowly.

'Excellent. That's settled, then.' Loukas's smile revealed his white teeth and reminded Belle of a predatory wolf. He was certainly as cunning, she thought grimly. 'Give me a list of the things you'll need for your workroom and I'll arrange for them to be delivered.'

His satisfied tone infuriated her. Loukas was king of his island and clearly used to always having his own way. She threw him a fulminating glance, which he returned with a mocking smile, but it was the gleam in his eyes, a silent reminder of the sexual attraction between them, that sent a frisson of unease down her spine. She had expected to stay on Aura for five days, but now she was committed to stay until the wedding. That meant five weeks of trying to fight her overpowering awareness of Loukas. It was no wonder her hand shook slightly as she picked up her glass of champagne and took a long sip.

The rest of the evening was torture for Belle as she struggled to hide her intense awareness of Loukas. She tried to relax and chat to Larissa, Georgios and his sisters, but all the time she was conscious of Loukas's speculative gaze, and she could not prevent herself from constantly glancing at him. She blushed when their eyes met, and hastily looked away, but even when she was not looking at him her body sensed when he was near and each of her nerve-endings quivered when she inhaled the spicy scent of his aftershave.

She did not know what to do—how to deal with her unexpected and utterly overwhelming attraction to him. It was terrifying and yet exciting. She had never felt this alive before. But her instincts were screaming danger. Loukas was too powerful, too strong-willed, and so out of her league. Maybe she should turn down the commission and go home? she thought wildly. Flee back to London and try to forget she had ever met Loukas Christakis.

She looked across the room to where Larissa was standing with Georgios, laughing at something he had said. She looked so happy, and was so excited about her wedding. How could she let her down? Belle thought heavily. And how could she consider giving up the most important commission of her career just because she was attracted to Larissa's brother? If only she could avoid him for the next few weeks, everything would be fine.

Larissa detached herself from her fiancé and crossed the room to speak to Belle. 'I'm returning to Athens with Georgios tonight. He's much more worried about

Constantine than he lets on, and I know he won't sleep in case there's a call from the hospital. If I promise to sit by the phone I may be able to persuade him to get a few hours' rest, and I'll come back first thing in the morning.' She looked anxiously at Belle. 'I'm sorry to leave you alone on Aura. Although of course you're not alone—Loukas is here,' she added, her face brightening. 'If you need anything, or have any problems, he'll be pleased to help.'

'I'm sure I'll be fine,' Belle murmured, refraining from mentioning that Loukas *was* the problem. She wished she could go to Athens too. The prospect of spending the night alone at the villa with him filled her with panic, but she managed to hide her inner turmoil and smiled reassuringly at Larissa.

After bidding everyone goodnight she returned to her room, and a few minutes later she heard the sound of the helicopter taking off. It seemed days rather than hours ago since she had left England. Now it was almost midnight, but she felt too keyed-up to go to bed, her mind returning inevitably to Loukas and how he had manipulated her to stay on Aura.

He was as domineering and forceful as her stepfather, she thought darkly. But that was not really true, her mind pointed out. It was obvious that he adored his sister, and she could not blame him for wanting to ensure that Larissa's wedding would be perfect. John Townsend had been a bully, but although Loukas was a powerful man he had a softer side to him, she acknowledged reluctantly. The tragic events in his life had made him hard and uncompromising, but he was fiercely protective of his sister, and beneath his tough exterior he must have a heart—a heart which, according to Larissa, had once been broken by the woman he had hoped to marry.

Belle knew she would never sleep while her brain was racing. She often worked late at night—for some reason it was her most creative time—so she slipped out of her room and made her way up to the top floor of the villa and along the hall to the room she was to use as a studio. On the way she passed the staircase which Larissa had told her led to the roof terrace, and after a moment's hesitation changed course and climbed the stairs.

At the top, an arched doorway opened onto a large roof garden, illuminated faintly by the silver gleam of the moon. It seemed as though you really could reach up and touch the stars, she mused, tilting her head to watch the countless glittering diamonds that studded the black velvet sky. The soft silence of the night air was broken only by the sound of an ornamental fountain, its fine spray of water droplets sparkling in the moonlight. A dining table and chairs were at one end of the terrace, but instead of sofas enormous cushions were piled on the floor beneath a draped voile canopy, the effect reminiscent of a Bedouin encampment.

It was so peaceful. Belle took a deep breath, her tension seeping away. But a voice from behind her had her wheeling around, and she gasped when she saw Loukas lounging casually in the doorway.

'I see you've discovered my hideaway,' he murmured softly.

She stared at him, her tension returning and exacerbated by his indolent air that plainly said he did not have a care in the world. Well, of course he hadn't. He'd got his own way. Loukas was in control of his kingdom and it was clear he regarded her as another of his puppets who would jump to his bidding. Anger flared inside her.

'I know the real reason why you're so determined that I should stay on Aura,' she challenged him, desperately trying to ignore her body's reaction to the fact that he had removed his jacket and tie and unfastened the top few buttons of his shirt to reveal an expanse of darkly tanned skin overlaid with black chest hairs.

His dark brows rose. 'Really? Why don't you enlighten me?'

'You still don't believe I am an experienced enough designer to make Larissa's wedding dress. That's why you want me here under your nose—so that you can keep checking on me. I've told you I'm prepared to work twenty-four hours a day if necessary to finish her gown and the bridesmaids' dresses in time for the wedding. Why don't you trust me?'

'Trust has to be earned,' he said abruptly, his jaw tightening as he walked towards her. He had trusted Sadie, Loukas thought grimly. Love had blinded him, and ultimately his faith in her had made a fool of him. His gut clenched as fetid memories of her treachery seeped like poison through his veins. He had grown adept at blanking out his bitterness, just as he blanked Sadie out of his mind. But he would never forget how she had betrayed him and the child she had been carrying—*his child*. The idea of trusting any woman ever again was laughable.

Belle tensed when Loukas halted a few inches from her. He was too close for comfort, but she was startled when she glimpsed a sudden bleakness in his eyes. He looked almost…vulnerable, and she felt a strong urge to slide her arms around him and hold him close.

His expression altered, hardened, and the moment passed. She must be crazy to think Loukas needed anyone, she told herself impatiently. His face was all angles and planes in the moonlight. His slashing cheekbones and square jaw could have been carved from granite, and the flash of pain she thought she had seen in his eyes must have been an illusion.

She shook her hair back from her face. 'I just want you to know that the *only* reason I've agreed to stay and make Larissa's dress here on Aura is because it will make life easier for *her*. There is so little time until the wedding, and I can see she is upset about Georgios's father.'

She made to step past him, but he caught hold of her arm and swung her back to face him, his eyes glinting when she gave him a furious glare.

'I owe you an apology.'

Her eyes widened, and the words, *Let go of me*, died on her lips. 'What do you mean?'

The moonlight had turned her hair into a silver river, streaming down her back, and her silvery dress shimmered, giving her an ethereal appearance. Loukas felt a piercing sensation through his heart—the same feeling he experienced sometimes when he watched the sun rise over the sea and he imagined that his father was out on his fishing boat.

For some reason beyond his comprehension Belle got to him in a way no other woman had done since Sadie. She was tiny and feisty and not afraid to stand up to him, and he found her a refreshing change from the simpering falseness of so many of his previous mistresses.

'I was wrong to take my anger with Larissa's first designer out on you,' he admitted. 'I am very protective of my sister and I was not prepared to risk her being hurt again.' He paused, his eyes roaming over Belle's slender figure, heat flaring inside him when he realised that she was bra-less beneath her dress. 'The evidence I've seen of your work proves that you are a talented designer. Your enthusiasm is obvious, as is your rapport with Lissa, and I'm pleased you are going to make her wedding dress.'

'Oh.' Belle was utterly taken aback by his apology. She had believed him to be as domineering as her step-father, but she had never known John to apologise for anything—not even his violent outbursts of temper which had so often resulted in the stinging slap of his palm across her cheek.

She studied Loukas's face, and felt a tightening sensation in the pit of her stomach as her gaze lingered on the sensual curve of his mouth. Her initial dislike of him had been a form of self-defence, she realised shakily. She was scared by the way he made her feel, shocked by her longing to feel his mouth on hers.

His hand was still on her arm, and a little shiver ran through her when he trailed his fingertips lightly up to her bare shoulder. His touch made her skin tingle, and her breath became trapped in her throat as her gaze meshed with his. No longer as hard as flint, his eyes burned with an undisguised hunger that evoked a primitive yearning inside her.

'Undoubtedly it will help Larissa if you make her dress here on Aura.' He paused, and the air between them seemed to tremble. 'But there is another reason why I want you to stay.'

His voice was as deep and soft as crushed velvet. Belle's heart jerked painfully against her ribs and she watched, paralysed, as his head slowly lowered and the moonlight was obscured. She licked her dry lips with the tip of her tongue. 'What…reason?' she whispered.

'This…'

He brushed his mouth over hers, capturing her surprised gasp as her lips parted helplessly. The kiss was slow and soft and unbelievably sensual, dragging her ever deeper into its passionate vortex. Pleasure exploded inside her with volcanic force. She trembled with a need that was beyond logical explanation, her body as taut as whipcord, a little moan escaping her when he tasted her again and again. She had wanted him to kiss her since she had watched him striding towards her on Kea. All day she had tried to deny her desire for him, but now it overwhelmed her in a torrent of sensation that she was powerless to resist.

The tasting became a lingering, sensual feast, a ravishment of her senses as he slanted his mouth over hers and deepened the kiss. His lips were firm, demanding her response, and it did not enter her head to deny him when this was what she wanted. His tongue traced the shape of her lips before probing between them. Dear heaven! His bold exploration took her to another level where conscious thought faded and instinctive response took over. She pressed her slender body up against the solid wall of his chest, and her breath left her in a rush when he closed his arms around her, one hand tangling in her hair and the other sliding up and down her spine.

Loukas was massively aroused. Belle could feel his rock-hard erection against her pelvis. But instead of bringing her to her senses the proof of his virility evoked a flood of molten warmth between her legs. This had gone too far, whispered a voice of warning inside her head. But her body refused to listen. All her life she had been sensible and obedient, forced to adhere to the rigid rules of her childhood. Maybe this was wrong, but she wanted Loukas with a ferocious need that was causing her whole body to tremble. How could it be wrong when it felt so right? her mind argued.

He should stop this now, before he lost control. Loukas lifted his head and stared down at Belle, the throbbing ache in his groin making a mockery of that thought. It had been too late from the moment his mouth had connected with hers. If he was honest, his self-control had been blasted apart from the moment he had caught sight of her petite figure on Kea, he acknowledged derisively.

No woman had aroused him this powerfully since Sadie. His jaw tensed. This was not the same. Although he hated to admit it, he *had* loved Sadie, and his desire for her had been more than just a physical urge. What he felt for the fragile blonde in his arms was nothing more than lust. Her eager response to him proved that she shared his hunger.

This was madness, Belle thought dazedly, unable to restrain a little gasp of pleasure when Loukas trailed his mouth over her cheek to her earlobe before following a moist pathway down her throat. Her entire body seemed to be one erogenous zone, her awareness of him so acute that she felt drunk on the exotic scent of his cologne. Her brain told her she should call a halt now, but the reasons for stopping him were no longer clear. Lucid thought was fading as an instinct as old as mankind took over.

'I want to see you.' His voice was rough—a deep rasp that ached with sexual hunger and evoked a primitive response in Belle. She trembled when he slid his hand to her nape and undid the hooks that secured the halter-neck top of her dress. Slowly, so slowly, he drew the silvery silk down, baring the creamy globes of her breasts inch by inch. She knew without looking down that her nipples had hardened into stiff peaks. He pulled the silk down to her waist and made a guttural noise low in his throat as he finally exposed the dusky pink crests that were jutting provocatively towards him, practically begging for him to touch them.

'*Theos*, you are exquisite.'

She caught her breath when he cupped her breasts in his palms, his skin enticingly warm against her flesh. The trembling in her limbs grew worse when he lowered his head and flicked his tongue across one nipple and then its twin, back and forth, over and over, until she gave a whimper of pleasure and her knees sagged. He caught her as she crumpled against him and swung her up into his arms so that for a few seconds the stars in the sky swirled like the endlessly reforming patterns in a kaleidoscope.

And then she was flat on her back, lying on the big floor cushions, the stars still visible through the sheer voile canopy above her. When Loukas knelt over her it seemed so natural that she ignored the whispered warning inside her head that he was all but a stranger. From the moment she had met him she had felt a fundamental connection with him that she could not explain, and when he leaned forward and claimed her mouth in a devastatingly sensual kiss the whisper of warning faded as desire pounded a pagan drumbeat through her veins.

Her lips felt swollen from the demanding pressure of his. But now his mouth was on her breast, and she cried out when he closed his lips around her nipple and sucked hard, sending starbursts of sensation shooting down to her pelvis. She never wanted the pleasure to stop, and pushed her fingers into his silky hair to hold him to his task as he transferred his mouth to her other breast. Reality faded. She stared up at the endless expanse of the night sky and felt adrift in the universe. She was free from her bullying stepfather, who had made her childhood a misery. She could do as she pleased, make her own decisions and live her life as she chose. The knowledge filled her with a heady sense of excitement.

Loukas was kneeling over her and she skimmed her hands over his chest, feeling the warmth that emanated from him. She wanted more, wanted to feel his naked skin beneath her fingertips, and in a fever of desire she tore open his shirt buttons and pushed the material over his broad shoulders. In the moonlight his skin gleamed like polished bronze. Eagerly she explored the defined muscles of his chest and abdomen. The mass of dark hair that arrowed down over his flat stomach and disappeared beneath the waistband of his trousers felt faintly abrasive against her palms. Driven by instinct, she brushed her fingers lightly over the distinct bulge straining against his zip and heard his harsh groan.

'Witch.' Loukas inhaled sharply, stunned by the realisation that he was on the brink of coming. His erection was hot and hard—*Theos*, so hard that his gut ached. He couldn't remember the last time he had felt this turned on. It was all he could do not to shove Belle's dress up, ease her panties aside and thrust his throbbing shaft into her.

He snatched a ragged breath as he stared down at her. She was more beautiful than a priceless work of art, with her long gold hair streaming over the cushions and her bare breasts creamy pale in the moonlight. She was a sorceress, and he was utterly captivated by her, entrapped by her spell, so that everything faded but his need to possess her. He wanted to see all of her, and his hands shook as he tugged her dress over her hips, the silk slithering through his fingers as he drew it down to expose her slender thighs.

Belle felt a moment of uncertainty when Loukas hooked his fingers into the waistband of her knickers. She had only met him for the first time earlier that day, whispered the voice of caution in her head. The feeling that she had known him for ever was an illusion. But she had learned a few things about him, her brain argued. She had discovered that he was a devoted brother and a loyal friend, and beneath his tough exterior he cared deeply about the people he loved. Her eyes met his, and her heart thudded at the determined intent in his gaze.

'You want this as much I do,' he told her, in his deep velvet voice that sent a shiver of response through her.

She could not deny it—did not want to discuss it or quantify it. She just wanted him, and the wanting was so strong, so intense, that nothing else in the universe mattered. She watched him mutely when he removed her final covering and slid his hand between her thighs. She allowed him to push her legs a little apart, and all the time her eyes were locked with his so that she saw the flare of satisfaction when he parted her with gentle fingers and discovered her slick wetness.

She could not restrain a little gasp of shock when Loukas found her ultra-sensitive clitoris, the gentle stroke of his thumb-pad across the tight bud causing her to arch her back as sensation ripped through her. She was burning up. Molten heat flooded between her thighs when he slid a finger inside her. Instinctively she thrust her hips forward, so that she could feel him go deeper still. Already tiny spasms were rippling low in her belly, but she wanted more—wanted him to fill her.

Driven by a level of need she had never experienced before, she clutched his shoulders and tried to force him down on top of her, but with a rough laugh he resisted. She whispered a protest when he eased away from her, and then gave a shiver of anticipation when she realised that he was stripping off his trousers and underwear. He was back within seconds, and her heart pounded at the feel of his hard thighs pressing against her pelvis. The tip of his erection pushed against her wet heat and she gasped at the size of him. Doubts formed in her dazed mind and she belatedly remembered her relative inexperience. It wasn't possible for her to take him. But he was easing forward slowly, as if he sensed her sudden trepidation. He slid his hands beneath her bottom, angling her to accept his penetration, and then he thrust deep and muffled her sob of pleasure with his lips as he captured her mouth in a drugging kiss.

Loukas's body was gripped by such a powerful need that he was overwhelmed by it, and his control was rapidly spiralling into the stratosphere. He began to move, slowly at first to allow Belle to accommodate him. Something told him that she had not done this very often, and he stifled his urgent need for sexual release so that the ultimate pleasure would be a mutual experience. But his resolve was tested by her eager response to him. Every stroke took him deeper within the velvet embrace of her body; every thrust took him closer to the edge. She matched his rhythm, arching her hips to him, her head thrown back against the cushions and her eyes half closed.

Nothing had prepared Belle for the intensity of pleasure Loukas was creating with every powerful thrust. He filled her, completed her, their two bodies joined as one and moving in perfect accord towards the magical place she sensed she was nearing. The stars above her glittered in the night sky before his dark head blotted them from her vision as he slanted his mouth over hers in a kiss that plundered her soul. She clung to him as the storm inside her grew ever stronger, and as the waves of pleasure built higher she urged him to increase his pace. She gave a sharp cry when her body suddenly convulsed in a mind-blowing orgasm that caused her internal muscles to clench and release over and over again.

He climaxed almost simultaneously, his hands gripping her hips as he effected one last devastating thrust and gave a savage groan, his face contorting in those moments of exquisite release before he slumped on top of her and snatched oxygen into his lungs. Belle could feel his heart thundering in time with hers, and tenderness swept over her that this big, powerful man had come apart in her arms. She pressed her lips to his cheek and silently acknowledged that she had never felt closer to another human being than she did at that moment. She wished they could stay like this for ever. It was her last conscious thought before sleep drew her down into its dreamless embrace.

CHAPTER SIX

THIS was not her room. Belle slowly sat up and stared around at the unfamiliar surroundings. Her brain slammed back into gear and she felt sick as her memory returned. *What had she done?*

A few moments ago, while cocooned in the blissful lethargy between sleep and wakefulness, she had been shocked by what she had assumed was a highly erotic dream. But she hadn't been dreaming. She had slept with Loukas last night. The spaciousness of the room and the vastness of the bed with its burgundy silk sheets indicated that this was the master bedroom. He must have carried her down here after they had had sex on the roof terrace.

Shame crashed over her in a tidal wave, and recriminations formed thick and fast inside her head. It was bad enough that she had slept with a man she had known for less than twenty-four hours. But to compound her stupidity it hadn't been any man—it had been Loukas Christakis, one of the most powerful businessmen in the world, who could crush her little company as easily as he could swat a fly if he chose.

He was a hardened cynic, and after his sister's first designer had turned out to be a crook he had been mistrustful of Belle and opposed to a relatively unknown designer making Larissa's wedding dress. But he had given her a chance and brought her to Aura—whereupon she had immediately dropped her knickers for him like a cheap tart.

Images taunted her of his naked body pressing down on hers, his mouth on her breast and his wickedly invasive fingers touching her intimately. In an agony of embarrassment she pressed her hands to her burning cheeks. She'd screwed up—literally, she thought grimly. No doubt Loukas was at this very minute arranging her departure from his island.

'Ah—you're awake. I was beginning to think you'd never stir.' He strolled into the bedroom through a door that Belle guessed led from the *en-suite* bathroom, looking every inch the suave business tycoon in a superbly tailored dark grey suit, crisp white shirt and navy tie. Belle was immediately conscious that she was naked, and clutched the sheet to her, her eyes wide and unknowingly wary as she tried to assess his mood. Would he shout at her in a furious rage, as John had so often done during her childhood, when he had accused her of some misdemeanour or other? Or would his anger be controlled and coldly sarcastic as he reviled her for her wanton behaviour?

Loukas walked over to the bed, and despite everything Belle's pulse-rate accelerated as she stared at his chiselled features, his smooth jaw an indication that he had recently shaved. He was so gorgeous that it was hardly surprising she had succumbed to his virile masculinity, but that was no excuse for what she had done, she acknowledged dismally.

'I know what you must be thinking,' she said

falteringly, wishing he hadn't lowered himself onto the edge of the bed so that the familiar scent of his aftershave teased her senses. 'I just want you to know that I have never done anything like…like last night before.'

Loukas frowned. 'Do you mean you were a virgin?'

She gave him a startled look. 'No—of course not, I had a relationship with a guy at university. Well, it wasn't a relationship as such—we were friends and ended up having a one-night stand.' She flushed, realising that she was waffling. 'It wasn't a good idea, really,' she mumbled, suddenly conscious that she had told Loukas more about herself than she had intended. 'Anyway, what I meant was that I've never…had sex…with someone only a few hours after meeting them.'

Did she have any idea how painfully vulnerable she seemed? Or how tempted he was to pull her into his arms and cover her tremulous lips with his mouth? Loukas wondered. Last night, as the moonlight had slanted silver beams over her slender body, he had thought that she could never look more beautiful. But this morning, with her blonde hair tangled around her bare shoulders and her mouth softly swollen from his kisses, she was a sleepy sex kitten, and his body was already hardening in anticipation of making love to her again.

He did not know why he was so pleased by her admission that she had only had one other lover. Her past was of no interest to him, and neither was her future, when in a few weeks from now their lives would take separate paths. All he was interested in was the present.

'Why does it matter if we had sex hours rather than days or weeks after we first met?' he queried coolly. 'It was going to happen at some point. The chemistry between us was white-hot from the minute we laid eyes on each other,' he insisted when she opened her mouth to deny it. 'Why wait when it was something we both wanted?'

'But we don't *know* each other!' Belle said shakily.

He shrugged. 'We know a few basic facts about one another, and we learned last night that we are extremely sexually compatible. What else do we need to know? It's not as if we're planning to spend the rest of our lives together,' he added sardonically.

For some reason his words evoked a little pang inside her. She had a sudden recollection of the moments after they had made love, when they had lain together while their breathing slowed and she had felt a sense of security—of belonging—that she had never felt in her life. Even before she had learned that John was not her real father she had felt like a cuckoo in the nest, she thought bleakly. But the idea that she somehow belonged with Loukas was ridiculous.

She glanced at him from beneath her lashes and her stomach contracted when she saw the feral desire in his eyes. Memories of his naked body descending onto hers, the feel of his rock-hard erection slowly penetrating her, caused a flood of honeyed moisture between her legs, and she instinctively tightened her grip on the sheet. Somehow she needed to regain control of the situation. It did not appear that Loukas was going to sack her, and from now on she was determined to focus on the job he had brought her to Aura to do.

'Well, anyway, it's certainly not going to happen again,' she said firmly.

'Of course it is,' he contradicted her smoothly. His arrogant self-assurance rankled, but before she could argue he leaned forward so that he was much too close for comfort. She shrank back against the headboard, her heart thudding when he placed his hands on either side of her head. His mouth hovered tantalisingly above hers, so that his warm breath whispered across her lips. 'One night wasn't enough for either of us. But I'm sure that by the time of Larissa's wedding we will have sated our desire for each other, and then we will both move on with our lives.'

Shock at what he seemed to be suggesting battled with shameful longing inside Belle's head. 'Are you saying you want us to have an affair while I'm staying on Aura?' she demanded.

'Can you think of a good reason why we shouldn't?' he countered equably. 'We're both consenting adults, free to do as we please. I'm not involved with anyone at the moment, and I assume you're not either?'

He was making it sound so simple—and maybe he was right, said a little voice inside her. Maybe she was looking for complications that didn't exist. Why *shouldn't* she have a brief fling with him? The sex last night had been indescribably wonderful. Admittedly she wasn't very experienced, but she knew instinctively that he had been as blown away as she had by the fiery passion that had blazed between them.

It was not as if there was any danger she would fall for him, she assured herself. He was not a bully, like her stepfather, but he was still too overpowering for her. The few men she had dated in the past had been gentle, artsy guys—sensitive and undemanding. Maybe a little boring, if she was honest, but she did not have time for grand passion when she needed to focus all her energy on establishing her business.

She chewed on her bottom lip. 'I need to concentrate on making the dresses in time for the wedding. And what would Larissa think?'

Loukas shrugged. 'I don't suppose she would care. The only problem is that my sister might view our relationship as a love-match. She's worried I'll be lonely once she has married Georgios and moved to Athens, and is keen for me to fall in love,' he explained, the biting irony in his voice a clue to his views on the subject. 'But there is no reason why she should even know. Lissa phoned earlier to say that Constantine underwent emergency heart surgery first thing this morning. Apparently everything went well, although he will remain in Intensive Care for several days. Larissa has decided to stay with Georgios at his family home in Athens so that they can visit his father. She'll fly back to Aura for dress fittings.'

That meant that she and Loukas would be alone at Villa Elena every night, Belle realised, catching her breath when he traced the delicate line of her collarbone with his finger and continued down to the valley between her breasts.

'Do you really want to lie in your lonely bed night after night, tormented by fantasies of my hands caressing your body?' he murmured. He tugged the sheet out of her nerveless fingers and his eyes glittered with sensual heat as he stared down at her naked breasts, her nipples as hard as pebbles. 'How many nights do you think you could resist the carnal hunger that consumes us both?'

Belle stared at him numbly, but he did not seem to need a reply—perhaps because he knew that she was incapable of resisting him, she thought, mortified by her weakness. But the truth was she couldn't resist him. She longed for him to kiss her, to roll her nipples between his fingers as he had done last night and create those exquisite sensations that she had only ever experienced with him. Disappointment swooped in her stomach when he suddenly stood up and strode across the room to the huge expanse of windows that ran the length of one wall and offered spectacular views of the sea.

'There *is* one other thing we need to discuss.' The sensual warmth had disappeared from his voice and he sounded terse, his body language no longer relaxed. 'I did not use a condom last night, so unless you are on the pill we had unprotected sex.'

Anger burned like acid in his gut—anger directed solely at himself. How could he have been so criminally careless? Loukas asked himself for the hundredth time since the truth had hit him like a blow to his solar plexus, forcing the oxygen from his lungs.

He had woken at dawn to find that Belle had moved from the side of the bed where he had lain her when he had carried her down to his room and was curled up against him, soft and warm, with her glorious hair spilling over the pillows. His arousal had been instant, but as memories of the passion that had exploded between them the previous night had flooded his mind so too had the shocking realisation that he had forgotten about contraception.

Self-loathing churned in his insides. Hadn't he vowed after Sadie had ended her pregnancy that he would take every possible precaution to prevent another woman accidentally conceiving his baby? He hadn't intended to make love to Belle on the roof terrace. But, like the sailors in the tales of Greek mythology his father had recounted to him as a boy, he had been lured by a siren and bewitched by her beauty. When he had taken Belle in his arms he had forgotten everything but his desire for her, and it did not matter how many recriminations he piled on himself, the stark truth was that she could now be pregnant.

He turned to face her, and the horrified expression on her face dashed his faint hope that she was on the pill.

'Oh, God! I didn't think…' The bottom dropped out of Belle's world. The possibility that she could be pregnant was too awful to contemplate. How would she manage? How would she be able to devote all her time to Wedding Belle if she had a child? 'It would be a disaster.' The words spilled from her—an instinctive reaction to a nightmare scenario. She did not notice Loukas's jaw tighten.

'I take it the idea of motherhood holds no appeal for you?'

There was a curious inflexion in his voice, but her mind was reeling from the potential consequences of the night she had spent with him and she did not pay it any attention. 'It certainly doesn't at this point in my life,' she admitted. 'I want to focus on my career—at least for the next few years.'

She knew it could take years to establish herself as a top designer. The truth was she doubted she would ever have children. She firmly believed that every child deserved to be brought up by both its parents, who preferably were married. But she did not want to get married and risk the unhappiness her mother had suffered with John. At twenty-five, she assumed she had years yet before her biological clock forced her to think seriously about whether she wanted to be a mother. But because of her irresponsible behaviour last night the decision might already have been made for her.

'When will you know if you have conceived?' Loukas asked grimly.

She made a hurried mental calculation and expelled a shaky breath. 'In a few days—but I think it will be okay. It's the wrong time of the month for me to fall pregnant.'

Loukas's expression was unfathomable. 'Let's hope so.' He walked back over to the bed and trapped her gaze, almost as if he was trying to see inside her head. 'I want to know. If you are pregnant it will be because of my negligence, and I will accept full responsibility.'

Something in his tone sent a little shiver through Belle. How would he react if she *had* conceived his baby? she wondered. And what did he mean when he said he would accept responsibility? For her? For the child? 'I'm sure it will be all right,' she said again, desperately trying to convince herself. The alternative was too difficult to think about.

He sat back down on the bed, and she swallowed when he slid his hand beneath her chin, tilting her head and holding her prisoner. 'I want you to give me your word that you will tell me if in a few days from now the situation is not as we both hope it will be.'

Was he acting out of concern? Or was this another example of his desire for control? She was finding it hard to think straight when he was so close, and she was disgusted with herself that even with the possibility of pregnancy hanging over her she longed for him to kiss her. She moistened her lower lip with the tip of her tongue, the gesture unknowingly inviting. 'I will tell you,' she assured him.

'Good.'

The rigid set of Loukas's shoulders relaxed a little, but a different tension filled him as he focused on Belle's reddened lips. He shouldn't be here. He was due at an important meeting. But instead of concentrating on business matters all he could think of was pushing aside the sheet to feast his eyes on Belle's slender body. And not just his eyes, he thought derisively. What was it about this woman that made him want to ignore his strong work ethic, and last night had made him abandon his principles of never having unprotected sex?

The distant sound of a helicopter approaching Aura jerked him to his senses. He had five weeks in which to satisfy his inconvenient desire for Belle, and forcing himself to wait until tonight to make love to her would heighten his anticipation. He lowered his head and captured her mouth in a brief, hard kiss, desire kicking in his gut at her eager response. It took all his formidable willpower to break the kiss, and he smiled at the flash of disappointment in her eyes.

'You'll have to be patient until tonight, my beautiful Belle. I have work to do—and so do you. Larissa's just arrived,' he told her, feeling a curious little tug inside him as he watched colour flare along her high cheekbones. For someone who described herself as a hard-headed businesswoman she seemed intriguingly unworldly. Belle was a potent mix of innocence and sensuality which he intended to enjoy for the next few weeks until Larissa's wedding.

* * *

Somehow Belle managed to act normally in front of Larissa, even though her mind was reeling from the events of the previous night. In the bright light of day she could almost convince herself she had dreamed the wild passion she had shared with Loukas on the roof terrace, but the slight sensitivity of previously unused muscles told their own story.

She blushed when she remembered how he had aroused her with his hands and mouth. He was an expert, a maestro in the art of making love, but no doubt he'd had plenty of practice, she thought ruefully. He had a reputation as a playboy and had often been pictured in gossip magazines with one glamorous mistress or another.

She couldn't imagine what he saw in *her*, for although she was averagely attractive Belle was well aware that she did not compare with the stunning supermodels Loukas favoured. But his desire for her had been urgent and demanding, and he'd made it clear that he wanted them to be lovers for the next few weeks while she was staying on Aura.

If she had any sense she would refuse. There were a hundred reasons why she should not have an affair with Loukas. But being sensible had never seemed less inviting, she admitted silently, as she bent her head over her sketchbook, where she was drawing her ideas for Larissa's dress.

There was no danger she would fall in love with him, she reassured herself. She did not need a man in her life; her career was all that mattered to her. But where was the harm in enjoying a few weeks of mind-blowing sex with a gorgeous Greek?

'Oh, that's *exactly* how I want my dress to look.'

Larissa said excitedly as she peered over Belle's shoulder and studied the sketch. 'I love the draped bodice and the long train.'

'I was thinking that the train should be made of Chantilly lace, and maybe the veil too,' Belle explained, forcing herself to concentrate on her designs. 'This is a sample,' she added, sifting through the piles of material that were spread across the table and handing Larissa a square of gossamer-fine white lace.

'It's perfect.' Larissa stood up and stretched. 'I think we've done enough for today. It's four o'clock. I hadn't realised we had been up here for so long.' A look of surprise crossed her face at the sound of a helicopter, and she glanced out of the window. 'I wonder why Loukas is back so early. Still, I'm glad he is, because his pilot can take me to Athens. Georgios's father is still in Intensive Care, but we can visit him for a few minutes this evening.' She hurried over to the door. 'I'll see you tomorrow, Belle.'

Down in the entrance hall of Villa Elena, Chip could not hide his surprise when Loukas walked into the house. 'You're home early, boss. Everything okay?'

'Why does everyone expect me to spend my life in my office?' Loukas growled, ignoring the fact that he often worked until eight or nine every night. His PA had been as shocked as Chip when he'd told her that he was finished for the day and not to put any calls through to him unless it was absolutely vital. 'I do have a life outside of work, you know. Where is my sister?'

'In the workroom with Belle—they've been up there all day—' Chip broke off when Loukas strode past him and took the stairs two at a time. He suspected there was a good reason why the boss was back so early—if the loaded glances between Loukas and Belle over dinner last night were anything to go by. Well, there was no denying that Belle was a looker, he mused. But he'd never known Loukas to put his interest in a woman before his dedication to running Christakis Holdings.

Belle was leaning over the table, adding the final details to the sketch she would work from when she made Larissa's dress. Engrossed in her work, she did not realise that she was no longer alone, and Loukas watched her for a few minutes, struck anew by her delicate beauty. Her pale hair fell in a silky curtain around her shoulders. He recalled how soft it had felt against his skin and his body instantly stirred as memories of making love to her the previous night assailed him.

She had been on his mind all day—a distraction he hadn't been able to ignore. For the first time in his life he had been bored during a business meeting to discuss his next big deal. He had found his thoughts straying to a beautiful blue-eyed blonde, and his impatience to have her again had intensified with every hour. Now he was back on Aura, and soon he would take Belle to bed, he thought with satisfaction, feeling his body harden in anticipation of sinking between her soft thighs.

Alerted by a slight movement, Belle lifted her head, and as her eyes locked with Loukas's enigmatic grey gaze she felt herself blush. So much for her decision to play it cool with him, she thought ruefully, hurriedly looking down at her sketch while she struggled for composure. She had been sure she could play the role of sophisticated mistress and indulge in a casual affair with him, but her desperate awareness of him as he strolled towards her made her feel like a naïve teenager rather than a *femme fatale*.

'How are you getting on?' he queried, coming to stand next to her so that he could study her drawings. 'I've just spoken to Larissa and she says you've almost finished the design for her dress.'

'Yes, we've done well today.' Belle's heart was thudding so hard she was sure Loukas must hear it. Unable to bring herself to look at him, she busied herself with tidying the work table, which was strewn with material samples and sheets of sketches. 'Tomorrow we'll start thinking about the bridesmaids' dresses, and then I'll take measurements and make paper patterns—'

She broke off when he slid his finger beneath her chin and tilted her face to his, and another wave of heat flooded her cheeks when she saw the sensual gleam in his eyes.

'Hey,' Loukas said softly. 'You don't have to give me a progress report. I have faith that you know what you're doing.'

He couldn't remember the last time he had seen a woman blush. After the explosive passion they had shared last night he had not expected Belle to be shy with him. He was used to mistresses who played the coquette and employed all their feminine wiles to keep him interested. But Belle had admitted that she had only had one other brief sexual encounter. Compared to the glossy, hard-as-nails socialites he usually dated, she seemed painfully innocent, and her vulnerability tugged on his insides.

'Lissa told me you went to see the church this morning,' he said, determinedly stifling the hormones that demanded he make love to Belle immediately.

Belle nodded. 'Yes, it's very picturesque,' she murmured, thinking of the tiny whitewashed chapel with its blue-domed roof, which had been built in the thirteenth century, according to the plaque on the wall. Set against a stunning backdrop of the sea, the ancient building had fired her imagination for the design for Larissa's dress.

'I was wondering if you would like me to give you a tour of the rest of Aura? I'll ask Maria to make up a picnic and we can stop off somewhere to eat.'

She gave him a startled glance and slowly released the breath that had been trapped in her lungs. She had never had an affair before, and had no idea of the rules, but it *had* occurred to her that all Loukas might want from her was sex. Her heart lifted at the realisation that he wanted to spend time with her outside of the bedroom. 'That would be great.' She smiled at him, unaware that the tentative gesture caused his gut to clench. 'I'd love to see your island.'

'Good.' Loukas tore his eyes from the rounded contours of her breasts, moulded so enticingly by her tight-fitting tee shirt, and resisted the temptation to lift her onto the table and ravish her. 'I'll see you downstairs in fifteen minutes,' he said as he strode over to the door, ruefully aware that he would spend most of that time taking a cold shower.

'Have you never ridden pillion on a motorbike before?' he asked a little later, when Belle walked out of the villa and eyed the bike doubtfully. 'There's nothing to it—just put your arms around my waist and hold on tight. I can see there are a lot of new things I'm going to have to teach you,' he added softly, his eyes glinting with amusement when she blushed again.

This relaxed, teasing side to Loukas was unexpected, Belle thought as she climbed onto the motorbike behind him. It would be very easy to fall for his lazy charm. But forewarned was forearmed, and she had no intention of allowing their affair to mean anything to her. There seemed to be nothing else to hold onto on the bike, and after a moment's hesitation she did wrap her arms around his waist, feeling the solid ridges of his abdominal muscles beneath her fingertips.

Riding pillion, with the warm air rushing past her face and her hair whipping out behind her, was terrifying and exhilarating. At first she squeezed her eyes shut, but it was clear that Loukas was in full control of the bike, and after a while she grew brave enough to look at the scenery flashing past. The narrow track which was the only road on Aura wound past olive groves and dense woodland, and skirted several tiny coves where white sand ran down to meet the turquoise-blue sea.

'This is the site of an ancient Greek temple,' Loukas explained when he stopped the bike by some stone ruins that were obviously centuries old. 'Possibly it was built to honour a goddess from Greek mythology. Aura was the goddess of the breeze and the fresh cool morning air. Presumably the island was named after her.'

'I'm fascinated by Greek mythology,' Belle admitted. 'The stories are so wonderful.'

'I'll lend you some books, if you like. I have dozens of them. My father knew many of the old tales and used to tell them to me when I was a boy.' A shadow crossed Loukas's face and Belle sensed his sadness.

'You must miss him, she said softly. She bit her lip, compelled to confide her own heartbreak. 'I know how it feels to lose a parent. My mother died three years ago and I miss her every day.'

His eyes met hers, compassion in his gaze. 'I'm sorry.'

The gentleness in his voice brought tears to Belle's eyes. 'Mum would have loved it here. There's a strange timelessness about the island.'

'Archaeologists from a museum in Athens believe there was a settlement here on Aura as long ago as the third millennium BC.'

'It's amazing to think people were here that long ago.' Belle stared around at the wild landscape. 'I love the fact that Aura is so natural and unspoilt.' She gave him a rueful look, remembering that his business was property development. 'I suppose you're going to tell me you have plans to build a huge hotel here, complete with golf course and amusement park?'

Loukas laughed. 'Not on your life. I love Aura's un-spoilt beauty too, and I intend for it to remain that way.' He stared curiously at Belle. 'Most women I know would only want to visit Aura if it had a five-star hotel with a spa, beauty salon and boutiques.'

Did that mean he thought she was unsophisticated? Belle glanced around the deserted beach they had reached via a narrow path leading down from the ruins, appreciating the rugged beauty of her surroundings. 'I guess I'm not like your other women,' she said cheerfully. 'Being alone here in this lovely place is my idea of heaven.'

'You're not completely alone,' Loukas reminded her. The sudden huskiness in his voice sent a quiver of anticipation down Belle's spine, and her heart leapt when he drew her towards him and ran his fingers through her hair. 'Do you want to swim in the sea?'

'I didn't bring my bikini,' she said regretfully. Her eyes widened when he grasped the hem of her shirt.

'You don't need it. As you pointed out, we're all alone. Have you never swum naked before?' he murmured, his breath whispering across her bare skin as he drew her tee shirt over her head and unclipped her bra. When she shook her head he grinned. 'I told you there were a lot of new experiences I was going to enjoy teaching you, my beautiful Belle.'

When he laughed he seemed younger, almost boyish, and his eyes were no longer like cold steel but gleaming with teasing amusement that turned to sensual heat as he dropped her bra on the sand and cupped her breasts. He lowered his hands to the zip of his jeans. 'Last one in the water is chicken.'

'Hey—that's not fair!' She had never seen a man strip out of his clothes so fast. She'd never seen a man strip, full stop, Belle acknowledged, struggling to drag her tight-fitting jeans down her legs. Loukas was already halfway down the beach, gloriously naked, his skin gleaming like polished bronze beneath the hot Greek sun. The sight of his taut buttocks and powerful thighs made Belle feel weak, and after a quick glance around the beach to make sure they really were alone she pulled off her panties and ran to join him.

The water was deliciously cool on her heated skin. 'I can't believe I'm doing this,' she said, gasping when strong arms closed around her waist and Loukas hauled her against his unashamedly aroused body.

'It's good, isn't it? To feel free and uninhibited?' He laughed and stroked her pink cheeks. 'I can't believe you're blushing again.' Their eyes held, and his laughter faded as he lowered his head and captured her mouth in a sensual kiss that tugged on Belle's soul.

It would be frighteningly easy to fall for him, she admitted when he carried her back up the beach and laid her on the rug he had spread out. But then he knelt over her, his big body blocking the sun, and as she pulled him down and wrapped her legs around his thighs conscious thought faded and she was swept away on a tide of sensation.

CHAPTER SEVEN

'THAT'S the last crystal in place, thank goodness.' Belle straightened up and flexed her aching shoulders. 'I thought I was never going to finish sewing them on, but it was worth the hours it's taken. The beaded bodice really adds a sparkle to the dress, don't you think?' She glanced at Larissa, eager to gain her reaction to the wedding dress now that it was finally completed, and was startled to see tears in the Greek girl's eyes.

'It's beyond words,' Larissa said huskily. 'Oh, Belle, it's so beautiful. It's so much more than I imagined from the sketches. It truly is my dream dress, and I can't thank you enough for all the work you've put into making it.'

'I'm glad you're happy with it.' Belle felt a sense of quiet pride. It was probably the best wedding gown she had ever created, she acknowledged as she studied the strapless dress of pure white silk tulle over a lace underskirt. The bodice and the edge of the full skirt were embellished with hundreds of crystals and tiny pearls. She had yet to sew crystals onto the veil, and with a week to go until the wedding she still had hours of work ahead to finish the bridesmaids' dresses.

'Loukas is home,' Larissa said, hearing the sound

of the helicopter. 'The pilot is going to take me back to Athens because Georgios's mother is holding a special dinner to celebrate Constantine being discharged from hospital. I'll send Loukas up to see my dress.' She gave Belle a speculative look. 'But I expect he'll come straight up to the studio anyway. He seems to enjoy spending time with you.'

Belle leaned down to flick an imaginary speck from the skirt of the dress, hoping Larissa would not notice her suddenly warm face. 'He's interested in how the dresses are progressing,' she mumbled.

'I have a feeling my brother is more interested in the designer than the dresses,' Larissa said dryly. 'For one thing, I've never known him to come home from work as early as he's been doing lately.'

'Perhaps he's not very busy at the moment.' The flush on Belle's cheeks suffused her whole body when she thought of how Loukas filled the hours that he was not at his office in Athens with making love to her. They had been discreet in front of Larissa—Belle had no more desire than Loukas to evoke his sister's matchmaking tendencies—but Larissa was clearly suspicious.

A fact that was confirmed when she said, 'Don't think I haven't noticed the way Loukas looks at you, or the way you look at him.' She grinned. 'I know something is going on between the two of you, and I think it's great. I'd *love* to have you as my sister-in-law, Belle. Maybe you will be designing your own wedding dress next?'

This had to stop right now. Belle shook her head firmly. 'No, that definitely won't happen.' She sighed when Larissa looked disappointed. 'I don't want to get married to anyone,' she explained. 'I'm far too busy running Wedding Belle. My career is more important to me than anything.' She hesitated. 'There's nothing between me and your brother.' At least that was a partial truth. Much easier than trying to explain that her involvement with Loukas was a purely sexual affair.

But then that wasn't strictly true either, she brooded, after Larissa had gone and she was left alone in the studio. Since she and Loukas had become lovers they had shared more than their fierce sexual desire for each other. Her mind drifted back over the long candlelit dinners and the lazy hours by the pool—after he had ignored her protests that she had to work and insisted she needed some relaxation time. They had explored the ancient ruins on Aura, and Loukas had taken her to Athens so see the Acropolis and other famous land-marks there after discovering that they shared an interest in ancient Greek history.

Her worry that she might have fallen pregnant that first time they had made love on the roof terrace had been dismissed when her period had started a few days later. Since then she had spent every night with Loukas, and their desire for each other, far from diminishing, seemed to grow ever more intense. Now there was only one week left until Larissa's wedding—one week before the end of their affair. For end it undoubtedly would. She knew that Loukas was flying to South Africa im-mediately after Larissa and Georgios departed on their honeymoon, and she needed to return to London— hopefully to a flood of new orders following the media coverage of Larissa's wedding.

Expelling a heavy sigh, she wandered over to the window and stared out over the vast expanse of the sea as blue as a sapphire, reflecting the cloudless sky above. She would miss the tranquil beauty of Aura. She bit her lip. Who was she kidding? She would miss Loukas. Much as she did not want to acknowledge the thought, it was the truth, and it settled like a lead weight in her chest. She hadn't fallen for him, of course, she assured herself. But all the same she hoped that the final week she spent on Aura would pass slowly.

'You look very pensive. What are you thinking about?'

Loukas had entered the studio silently and, seeing that Belle was lost in her thoughts, had paused for a few moments to study her. If possible she was even more beautiful than when she had arrived on Aura, he mused. Her long hair, hanging in a braid down her back today, had turned even blonder from the Greek sunshine, and she had gained a light golden tan which made her eyes seem even bluer. Desire ripped through him, but something about her solitary stance tugged on his insides. Sometimes she seemed to close in on herself, and not for the first time he sensed an air of sadness about her that made him want to take her in his arms and simply hold her close.

She turned at the sound of his voice and flashed him a breezy smile that he noticed did not reach her eyes. 'I was thinking about how many crystals I still have to sew onto Larissa's veil. Her dress is finished, thankfully. Would you like to see it?'

He pushed away the thought that what he would like to do was break down the barriers she hid behind and discover the real Belle Andersen. Why was he curious? he asked himself irritably. She was his temporary mistress and a week from now he would probably never see her again. He frowned, wondering why the prospect seemed so unappealing.

'Of course I want to see the result of your long hours of hard work.' She was often in the studio before he left for his office every morning, and some evenings he had to frogmarch her downstairs and insist that she eat her dinner. She wasn't so much hard-working as obsessive. He tensed at the thought. Who did *that* remind him of?

In his mind he pictured Sadie, when they had both been eighteen and living in the same tenement block in New York. He had been scraping a living running the grocery store, and Sadie had been a student at a performing arts college, long before her ascent to fame.

'I can't see you any more, Loukas. I have to spend every minute of my free time practising. Dancing is my life, and one day my name is going to be in bright lights on Broadway.'

His mind fast-forwarded twelve years. The venue was his luxurious Manhattan penthouse. Sadie was the darling of Broadway and an international star, and they had been having an affair for a year.

'I can't have a baby, Loukas. It would be the end of my career. Performing is my life, and I can't take months off and risk losing my figure.'

He had given his heart to Sadie, and she had ripped out his soul, he thought savagely. Now his heart was as impenetrable as a lump of granite, and he had no intention of falling in love again. His relationship with Belle was just another enjoyable but ultimately meaningless affair, he assured himself as he strolled across the studio.

Belle removed the dust sheet covering Larissa's dress. 'Well, what do you think?' she asked anxiously, after several seconds had ticked past and Loukas remained silent.

'I did you a serious injustice when I doubted your skill as a designer,' he said quietly. 'The dress is exquisite. Lissa has told me how delighted she is with it. There is no doubt in my mind that Wedding Belle has a great future.'

Belle flushed with pleasure at his praise. Loukas's words were like a healing balm after the scorn with which John Townsend had greeted her early design work.

'You're wasting your time applying to art school. You don't have any talent.'

He had seemed to take pleasure in mocking her dreams, she remembered painfully. For years she had wondered why he did not love her, and had concluded that it must somehow be her fault. Now she knew otherwise. She would never know her true identity, Belle accepted, but running her own company gave her a sense of identity. Wedding Belle was more than a business: it was the most important thing in her life.

She smiled at Loukas. 'I hope you're right. I'm prepared to work hard and devote all my time and energy to making Wedding Belle a success.'

A curious expression crossed his face, but it was gone before she had time to wonder about it. 'In that case we had better make the most of your remaining time on Aura, before you leave to take the fashion world by storm,' he drawled softly. His sensual smile stole her breath and her pulse quickened when he ran his hand lightly up her bare arm. 'Are your shoulders aching again?'

She closed her eyes blissfully when he stood behind

her and began to massage the knot of muscles at the base of her neck. 'Mmm…that feels good. I am a bit stiff.'

He gave a low chuckle, his warm breath fanning her ear as he pulled her up against him. 'So am I, my beautiful Belle—and not just a bit.'

'Yes…I can feel,' she said breathlessly. Molten heat pooled between her thighs as she felt the solid length of his arousal nudge the cleft of her bottom through her thin cotton skirt. Desire thundered through her veins. Their clothes were a frustrating barrier and her heart thudded when he tugged the straps of her top down her arms so that her breasts spilled into his hands. 'Loukas, I need to work…' It was a token protest which he ignored as he brought another gasp from her by rolling her nipples between his fingers until they stiffened to taut, tingling peaks.

Pleasure seared a path down Belle's stomach to her pelvis, and she offered no protest when he turned her to face him. 'You need this,' he told her assuredly. 'And so do I, Belle *mou*.'

His mouth captured hers in a deep, drugging kiss, seducing her senses so that she was only aware of the musky scent of his aftershave and the faint abrasion of his jaw against her cheek. How could she deny her need for him when it consumed her and caused her limbs to tremble?

When he lifted her into his arms she rested her head on his shoulder, her heartbeat quickening with every stride he took along the hallway to the master bedroom. *One more week*—the words beat dully inside her head and filled her with an urgency to snatch the days and hours she had left with him. He lowered her onto the bed and she wound her arms around his neck to draw him down beside her.

Loukas gave a rough laugh as he fought a losing battle to control his hunger for this fragile blonde who had become a serious addiction. He loved her eagerness and delighted in her unrestrained passion, in the little cries of pleasure she made when he stripped off her skirt and knickers and pressed his mouth to the moist opening between her thighs. With exquisite gentleness he explored her with his tongue, until she arched her hips in mute supplication for him to take her to the magical place that was uniquely theirs.

He would miss her. The thought slid into his head as he stood to remove his own clothes, his eyes never leaving her as he watched the rays of sunlight filtering through the blinds gilding her slender body. He briefly considered asking her to remain as his mistress for the next month or two, or however long it took before he grew bored of her—as he undoubtedly would, he assured himself. But he dismissed the idea. Business would keep him in South Africa for at least a month, and he knew Belle was impatient to return to London, hopeful that Larissa's wedding would generate interest and new orders for her company.

He had one more week to enjoy her, and he intended to do just that, he vowed as he swiftly donned protection and positioned himself over her. Her smile evoked a curious tugging sensation on his heart, but as he eased forward and entered her with one deep thrust his mind closed down and he was aware of nothing but the velvet grip of her body's embrace and the pounding of his blood in his veins. He withdrew almost fully and then thrust again, deeper, faster, the sound of his ragged breath mingling with her soft moans as she matched his rhythm and their bodies moved together in total accord, reached the heights, and shattered in the ecstasy of simultaneous release.

The wedding had been a fairy tale; there was no other word to describe it, Belle thought afterwards. Larissa had looked breathtaking in her wedding gown, and the bridesmaids had been equally stunning in dresses of palest pink taffeta which matched the bride's bouquet of pink rosebuds and the groom's buttonhole.

Georgios had looked handsome, and a little nervous, but the expression on his face when he had smiled at his bride had evoked an inexplicable ache inside Belle. She wasn't envious, she assured herself. She was quite certain that she never wanted to get married. But to be loved as much as Georgios clearly loved Larissa and to be able to return that love without fear of being hurt or rejected must be a wonderful thing.

Suddenly restless, she jumped up from her bed, closed the zip of her suitcase and walked over to the window. The evening sunlight was mellow and golden, and the scent of lemons drifted up from the grove beneath her room. She had fallen in love with this place, she thought with a sigh: the villa, the island…Loukas. Her heart jerked against her ribs. Of course she hadn't fallen for Loukas—it was just that her imminent departure from Aura was making her stupidly emotional.

He was leaving too. His flight to Cape Town was due to leave Athens an hour after her return flight to London, and in a few minutes they would make the journey to the mainland on his private helicopter.

Her mind turned back to the wedding. There had

been a gasp from the congregation when Larissa had entered the church, but Belle's eyes had been fixed on Loukas as he had proudly escorted his sister down the aisle. He had been a surrogate father to Larissa since she was a little girl, and had shouldered the responsibility of bringing her up after the death of their parents, when he had been so young himself.

As the service had begun Belle had glanced at his hard profile. His expression had revealed nothing of his private thoughts, but she had sensed instinctively that he was fighting to control his emotions as his sister left her old life and started out on a new journey with her husband. Without pausing to question what she was doing she had reached out and clasped his hand, trying to tell him with actions rather than words that she understood and sympathised with how he must be feeling.

For a few seconds Loukas had stiffened, and she had been prepared for him to reject her. But then he had gripped her fingers tightly and glanced down at her up-turned face. Something had flared in his eyes, but faded before she was able to assimilate it. She had given him a tentative smile, and in response he had squeezed her hand and held it captive in his own for the remainder of the service.

Forcing her mind back to the present, she checked her watch and saw that it was time to go. The rest of the day had been madly hectic as four hundred guests had filed into the huge marquee erected in the garden of Villa Elena for the reception. Loukas had been so busy with his duties as host that she had barely spent any time with him. And now it was too late. The dull ache in Belle's chest intensified as she carried her case downstairs to the main hall.

'Hey, I was just coming to get that for you.' Chip, impeccably smart in his butler's uniform, greeted her. 'The boss is waiting for you on the pad.' He picked up her case and preceded her down the front steps. 'I hope you're going to come and visit Aura again, Belle.' He slanted a sideways glance at her and added quietly, 'Loukas keeps his thoughts private, and he can be hard to get to know, but he's a great guy—one of the best. I reckon he's going to be lonely with Larissa and you both gone.'

'I don't suppose a good-looking billionaire will remain lonely for long,' Belle said drily. The ache inside her became a searing pain as she imagined Loukas making love to another woman. 'I bet he has hundreds of girlfriends,' she muttered.

Chip shrugged, but did not deny it. 'He's never brought any of them to stay on Aura, though.' He paused and gave her another speculative look. 'Apart from you.'

Belle coloured. Of course Chip was aware of her affair with Loukas. It must have been pretty obvious that for the past month she had never slept in her own bed. But what did it matter? She was leaving now, and she was sure Chip knew as well as she did that she wouldn't be coming back to the island. It was a well-documented fact that Loukas's affairs never lasted long.

He was standing by the helicopter, his tall figure silhouetted against the setting sun. She drank in the sight of him greedily, wanting to impress his handsome features indelibly on her mind. He had changed out of the formal suit he had worn for the wedding into beige chinos and a black polo shirt, and looked relaxed and so utterly gorgeous that she felt a sharp pain pierce her like an arrow through her heart.

'All set?'

His sunglasses shielded his eyes. She wanted to snatch them from him so that she could look for one last time into his slate-grey gaze. But perhaps it was better this way, for if he looked into her eyes he would surely see the tears she was fighting to hold back.

'Yes, I'm ready to leave.' Somehow she managed to sound convincing, even cheerful. 'Larissa and Georgios should already be on their way to the Maldives. What a wonderful venue for their honeymoon.' She bit her lip when he helped her step up into the helicopter and she breathed in the familiar spicy fragrance of his cologne mingled with another subtly masculine scent that was uniquely his. It was imperative that she kept on talking, before her composure cracked and she begged him to allow her to stay with him.

'I had a call from Jenny, my office manager, who has been manning things at Wedding Belle while I've been away,' she chatted brightly as she sank down into a plush leather seat and fastened her safety belt. 'Apparently photos of Larissa's dress have already been posted on the internet, and we've received dozens of enquiries by email.'

'Good,' Loukas replied in a clipped tone. Just as he had predicted, Belle clearly could not wait to get back to London and her business. When she had walked towards the landing pad, dressed in the elegant cream and black silk skirt and jacket she had been wearing the first time he had seen her on Kea, he had once again been tempted to ask her to come to South Africa with him. He was glad now he had hesitated. It would have been embarrassing for both of them. No doubt he'd soon forget her once he was involved with the new project in Cape Town, he told himself.

By the time the helicopter had dropped them at Athens airport and they had made their way through the crowds to the check-in desks Belle's flight number had flashed up on the screen, indicating that it was time to walk through to her gate ready for boarding. Loukas had seemed remote since they had left Aura, and from the various phone calls he had made on his mobile she guessed his mind was already focused on his business trip.

'Well…' She dredged up a brilliant smile, pride her only ally against the tears that were hovering perilously close. 'I guess this is goodbye.' What on earth was she supposed to say to him? she thought desperately. They had been lovers for the past month and it was only now, when she was facing the fact that she might never see him again, that she admitted how much she would miss him. 'If you're ever near the river in south-west London and you happen to see a houseboat called the *Saucy Sue*, come onboard and say hello.'

His dark brows lifted quizzically. 'Your boat is called *Saucy Sue*?'

'My brother named her. Don't ask.' This was hell. Loukas plainly did not give a damn that they were un-likely to ever see each other again, while she cared way too much. She flashed him another smile and checked in her handbag for her boarding pass for the hundredth time. 'Goodbye, Loukas.'

'You don't think I'd let you go that easily, do you?' His sexy smile stole her breath and his lazy words made her heart leap. Maybe he wasn't going to let her go at all? She trembled when he slid his hand beneath her chin and tilted her face to his. The brush of his mouth over hers instantly transported her to heaven and she parted her lips for him to deepen the kiss. But almost immediately he lifted his head. The disappointment was crushing, excruciating, and for a moment she could not breathe as he released her chin and stepped back from her.

Loukas stared down at Belle, memories of the past weeks they had spent together flooding his mind. The passion they had shared had been electrifying, but there had been so much more than that, he acknowledged. He had enjoyed simply being with her, taking her for rides on his motorbike, swimming with her in the sea, and they had talked for hours.

He hadn't expected that saying goodbye to her would be this hard. But there was no alternative. Belle's life was in England, where she ran her business, and his was in Greece. A long-distance affair would be unsatisfactory, and he wasn't looking for a relationship, he reminded himself. His jaw hardened and he forced himself to turn away from her. '*Antio*, Belle. And good luck with Wedding Belle.'

And then he was gone, striding through the crowd with his natural grace, his height making him easily visible. Belle watched him go, willing him to turn his head, to give one last wave of his hand, but he did not look back.

She remained staring across the vast foyer long after he had disappeared from view. She had always known their affair was a temporary arrangement, she reminded herself. It was for the best. She could not focus on developing Wedding Belle if she was involved with Loukas. When she was with him he filled her thoughts to the exclusion of everything else, and if she was going to follow her dream of being a top designer she could not allow herself to be distracted by anyone.

Three weeks later, Belle stared dazedly at her GP. 'I *can't* be pregnant,' she said shakily.

'According to the test, you conceived approximately eight weeks ago,' the doctor told her. 'Do you remember if you had unprotected sex then?'

'Only once,' she admitted. But of course once was all it took, she thought sickly. 'But I had my period a few days later.' She recalled how relieved she had been. It was true her period had been lighter than usual, but they had never been heavy, and she had been thankful that her irresponsibility that first time she had slept with Loukas had not had any consequences.

She had only visited the doctor at her brother's insistence because she had been feeling constantly tired since she had returned from Greece. She hadn't really expected anything to be wrong. It was not surprising she was tired when she had been spending up to ten hours a day at the studio, as she'd reminded Dan. The media exposure from Larissa's wedding had triggered huge interest in Wedding Belle, and she had been determined to make the most of this opportunity to establish herself as a designer.

'Some women experience bleeding in the early months of pregnancy,' the doctor explained. 'But it isn't a proper period and it often stops as the pregnancy progresses. And not all women ovulate around the middle of their cycle. For some it happens earlier or, as must have happened in your case, later.'

'You have to tell Christakis,' Dan insisted when she

broke the news to him. 'He is the baby's father and he has a duty to help you—financially at least. Let's face it, he can afford to,' he added fiercely, when Belle looked as if she was going to argue. 'You can't bring up a child on your own. How are you going to work with a baby in tow? And where will you live? I'm afraid *Saucy Sue* won't survive another winter without major work on her hull. And anyway, a houseboat is no place to bring up a baby.'

'You're not telling me anything I haven't already gone over in my mind a hundred times,' Belle said bleakly, hugging her arms around her body as if she could some-how protect herself from the nightmare that was unfold-ing. She still could not take it in. She was expecting Loukas's baby. It was crazy, unbelievable, but since her visit to her GP, scarily real. 'I don't know what to do,' she admitted shakily.

She had no idea how Loukas would react to the news that she had conceived his child as a result of their care-lessness the first time they had slept together. He had certainly appeared to share her relief when she had in-formed him that her period had started. No doubt he would be as shocked as she was.

'You don't have to go through with it, Belle.' Dan sounded hesitant and carefully avoided her gaze. 'I'll support any decision you make.'

She swallowed the lump in her throat. Her brother's loyalty meant so much to her. But Dan's words broke through the sense of numbness that had enveloped her and forced her to face up to the reality that she was expecting a baby. A new life was developing inside her and was totally dependent on her for its survival. It was a humbling thought, and she was shaken by the feeling of fierce protectiveness that swept through her.

'If Mum had terminated her unplanned pregnancy twenty-five years ago I wouldn't be here,' she said huskily. 'I can't make the baby pay for my mistake.'

'It's Christakis's mistake too,' Dan said tautly.

'What if I tell him, and he accepts responsibility for his child but resents it—like John resented me?' Belle voiced her greatest fear.

'This is different. You know now that John isn't your biological father. When we were growing up you were a living reminder that Mum had been unfaithful to him. It wasn't your fault, and it was unforgivable that he took his bitterness out on you,' Dan muttered grimly. 'But you are carrying Christakis's child—his flesh and blood.'

Dan's words tore on Belle's fragile emotions. How could she deny her child its father and keep his identity a secret, as her mother had done to her? Since she had learned the truth of her parentage she had felt as though she was half a person, she thought painfully. She wasn't a Townsend, like Dan, but she wasn't really an Andersen; she had just taken her mother's maiden name to distance herself from John. She would never know who she was, or whose blood ran through her veins. How could she inflict that same uncertainty, that feeling of not belonging anywhere, on her baby?

'I've got to go.' Dan's voice broke into her thoughts. 'I'll be away on the photoshoot for a couple of days.' He slung his backpack over his shoulder, leapt off the boat onto the towpath and paused to look back at her. 'You *have* to tell Christakis.'

'I know,' Belle said heavily. In her heart she accepted

that Dan was right. For the baby's sake she had a duty
to tell Loukas she was carrying his child.

But finding the courage to inform Loukas of her pregnancy was easier said than done. Several times she
brought up his mobile number on her phone but could
not bring herself to make the call. She knew he was
still in South Africa and decided to delay telling him
her news until after her ultrasound scan, which would
determine when the baby was due.

On the morning of her hospital appointment she
struggled to do up the zip on a dress that had fitted
perfectly only a couple of weeks ago. Now it was uncomfortably tight across the bust and hips, and when
she turned sideways to the mirror she could see a small
but distinct mound instead of her usually flat stomach.
Surely it was too early for her pregnancy to be showing?
Tears stung her eyes as panic overwhelmed her. She
didn't want her life to change irrevocably, and more
than anything she did not want to sacrifice her dream
of making Wedding Belle a successful business.

The sound of footsteps on the deck above told her
that Dan was home from his trip. Blinking away her
tears, she fitted one of her earrings and cursed when
she dropped the other and it rolled under the table.

'I suppose an estate agent's description of a houseboat
would be "cosy and compact".'

On her hands and knees, at the sound of a familiar
male voice that definitely did not belong to her brother
Belle jerked her head up so that her skull met the un-
derside of the table with a sickening thud.

'*Theos*! Be careful. What are you doing down there

anyway?' Strong hands gripped her arms and gently drew her to her feet.

Belle stared in dazed disbelief at Loukas's darkly handsome face, and a wave of dizziness swept over so that she had to cling to the edge of the table for support.

'Wh…what are you doing here?' She could barely speak, her voice emerging as little more than a whisper as shock ricocheted through her. 'Did Dan phone you?'

Loukas frowned. 'Why would your brother call me?'

'I…I don't know.' Belle clutched her pounding head. 'I'm not thinking straight. It's just such a surprise to see you.' She almost laughed at the understatement and drew a ragged breath. *'Why are you here, Loukas?'*

CHAPTER EIGHT

IT WAS A question he had asked himself many times, Loukas acknowledged derisively. *Why* had he pushed through the project in South Africa at record speed, even though it had meant working up to eighteen hours a day? And *why* had he flown straight to London rather than Athens?

Until a few moments ago he had not had an answer, and even now he did not understand exactly what he wanted from his relationship with Belle. But one thing had become clear the second he had laid eyes on her. He wanted her. His desire for her had not faded during the weeks they had been apart, and he finally accepted that his foul mood while he had been in South Africa had been because he missed her.

Somehow this petite, beautiful blonde had crept under his skin. She looked even better in the flesh than in his fantasies, and a little more curvaceous, he noted, his eyes lingering on the rounded fullness of her breasts beneath the lilac silk dress. But she was clearly startled by his visit, and the wariness in her eyes held him back from pulling her into his arms and claiming her mouth.

'I had to come to London on business,' he lied, 'and

decided to take a stroll by the river. Out of interest, why do you live on a houseboat?'

'Dan and I both need to live in London for work, and the rent here is cheaper than on a flat,' Belle explained distractedly. Her initial shock at his unexpected appearance was fading and the pounding sensation in her ears had nothing to do with hitting her head. She had believed she would never see him again. But Loukas was here, looking utterly gorgeous in a lightweight grey suit and a pale blue shirt which was open at the throat so that she could glimpse the dark hairs that she knew covered his muscular chest. Just one look was all it took for her to fall under his spell. He seduced her senses with one smile, and as her eyes focused on his mouth everything faded from her mind but her aching longing for him to kiss her.

'Belle…?' His voice roughened, and his eyes narrowed and gleamed with a feral hunger that made her tremble. Her breath hitched in her throat when he brushed her hair back from her face and cupped her cheek in his palm, stroking his thumb-pad lightly over her lips. Instinctively she parted them as his dark head descended.

'Belle—are you down there? I'm back…'

The violent intrusion of her brother's voice jerked Belle to her senses and she stepped back from Loukas, breathing hard. Dan walked slowly down the steps from the upper deck, his eyes locked on the tall man at his sister's side. 'You must be Christakis,' he said tersely. 'I suppose it's to your credit that you came as soon as Belle told you about the baby.'

The ensuing silence screamed with tension. Loukas could hear his blood roaring in his eardrums. Every muscle in his body clenched and his lungs froze so that he could not breathe or speak. Slowly he turned his head from the scruffy, long-haired young man who was eyeing him aggressively to Belle, whose eyes were great, dark orbs in her white face. '*Thee mou*! What baby?' he demanded hoarsely.

'Oh, hell!'

Whipping his head round, Loukas glared at the unknown intruder. 'Who are you?' Belle had told him she lived with her brother, but there was no physical resemblance between her and this man. Rage seared his insides at the idea that the man could be her lover.

Belle spoke first. 'This is my brother,' she said shakily. She gave Dan a pleading look. 'Could you give us a few minutes?'

Dan hesitated, clearly doubtful. 'Are you sure?'

'Yes.' She bit her lip. 'Loukas and I need to talk.'

As soon as Dan had gone Loukas's hard-as-flint gaze flicked back to her, and she shivered at the icy expression that had replaced the warmth of only a few seconds ago when he had been about to kiss her.

'I was going to tell you,' she said quickly. 'I…I was going to phone, but you were in South Africa…' Her voice tailed away as she watched his face harden so that he looked as though he had been carved from granite.

'*You're pregnant?*' Shock caused his voice to emerge as a harsh rasp. 'How can that be when you told me you had not conceived after the one and only time we failed to use protection?' He paused, his brain whirling. 'Why did you lie? Was it because you did not want me to know that you had conceived my child?'

He was reliving a nightmare, Loukas thought grimly. Three years ago Sadie had kept her pregnancy a secret from him, and the only reason he had found out was because she had been rushed into the hospital after collapsing on stage during a performance and the truth had come out.

'I didn't tell you because I don't want the baby.' Sadie's words returned to haunt him. Had Belle kept her pregnancy a secret from him for the same reason?

'I did not lie,' Belle defended herself urgently. 'I had what I assumed was a period. But it turns out that I was mistaken…'

Once again her voice faltered at Loukas's sardonic expression. She had been prepared for his anger, but she was still hurt by it. They had both been careless that night, but he clearly blamed *her*, she thought bitterly.

'I have to go,' she muttered, catching sight of the time. 'I have a hospital appointment this morning. We can talk when I get back.'

Loukas's blood ran cold as memories of Sadie's treachery tormented him. He remembered the look of horror on Belle's face when she had realised she might have fallen pregnant the first time they had slept together. She had made it quite clear that she did not want a child while she was busy developing her dress design business. 'Why are you going to the hospital?' he demanded harshly.

'I'm due to have an ultrasound scan.' Belle bit her lip. 'To tell you the truth, I'm nervous,' she admitted. 'I'm struggling with the idea of having a baby, and I don't know how I'll feel when I see the evidence that my life is going to change for ever.'

Her honesty was one of the traits he most admired about her, Loukas thought, the fierce tension that had gripped him easing a little. Sadie had gone behind his back and had a termination without telling him. She hadn't given him a chance to prove that he would be supportive during her pregnancy and she had denied him his child.

Now Belle was expecting his baby. Myriad emotions stormed through him as the news sank in. He had been given another chance to be a father. *Theos*, his disbelief was turning to amazement and a fierce joy was expanding inside him, filling every pore. He knew without a shadow of doubt that he wanted this child—but what about Belle? She was clearly scared and uncertain of the future.

He expelled a long breath and crossed the tiny living space of the houseboat to stand in front of her. 'Both our lives will change,' he told her quietly. 'We are in this together, Belle. We might not have planned to have a child, but you are carrying my baby and I will be with you every step of the way.'

She was glad Loukas was here, Belle thought, as she lay on a narrow bed wearing an unglamorous gown that was rolled up to expose her stomach. She had never been in a hospital before—at least, not as a patient.

She tried to blank out the memories of waiting in the A&E unit her mother had been taken to after the car accident, of the doctor walking towards her and taking her hands in his as he had gently broken the news that Gudrun was dead. The smell of disinfectant was a painful reminder of that terrible day. She suddenly felt panicky and claustrophobic in the small, dark room where she was about to have the scan, but as if he sensed her tension Loukas enveloped her hand in his much bigger one and lightly squeezed her fingers.

'Try to relax.' His deep voice was reassuring, and for some stupid reason tears filled Belle's eyes. She wished they were like the other couple they had met in the waiting room, who were obviously deeply in love and excited to be expecting their first child. Loukas had promised to support her during her pregnancy, but the stark truth was that their affair had ended weeks ago and this baby was unplanned.

The sonographer had already smeared gel onto Belle's stomach, and now she moved the sensor slowly over her abdomen. 'Here we are,' she said as a grainy image appeared on the screen. 'This is your baby—can you see the heart beating?'

To Belle's eyes it looked like an indistinct blob. It was hard to believe that that tiny fragile pulse was the beating heart of a new life—her baby. 'It's real, then?' she said faintly. She spoke the words unconsciously. A host of emotions was swirling inside her, chief of which, right now, was fear at the enormity of what was happening to her. She wasn't ready to have a child. She didn't know how she was going to manage.

She darted a glance at Loukas, wishing that he was still holding her hand. But he was leaning forward, his eyes focused intently on the screen, and she had no clue from his tense profile what he was thinking. Was he angry that he was caught in a situation he had not asked for? she wondered, biting her lip. He was used to being in control, used to every aspect of his life running with smooth efficiency. Did he resent being unable to control fate?

The sonographer smiled sympathetically. 'You're not alone. Lots of women find it a shock when they first see the evidence of their pregnancy. The scan makes it more real.' She paused. 'I have something else to tell you that might be even more of a shock.'

'Is there something wrong with the baby?' Loukas tore his eyes from the screen and stared at the sonographer, his jaw rigid as he fought to control the emotions that had surged through him when he had seen the beating heart of his child.

As far as he knew Sadie had not had a scan. Perhaps if she had, if she had seen the fragile life growing inside her, she would have allowed her pregnancy to continue. But all she had cared about was her career, he thought bitterly. The child she had conceived by him had been an inconvenience which she had discarded, uncaring of his feelings. He would never forget the pain that had ripped through him when she had admitted what she had done, the guilt that somehow he should have done more to convince Sadie to go ahead with her pregnancy. But she had undergone a termination without his knowledge the day after he had discovered she was carrying his baby.

'Everything looks as it should at this early stage,' the sonographer explained. She hesitated. 'But there are two embryos. You are expecting twins,' she told Belle gently.

This could not be happening. Belle stared blankly around the small, bare-walled cubicle where she had come to change back into her clothes and wondered if she was going mad. She did not remember much of what the sonographer had said after the word *twins*, although she vaguely recollected her explaining that the babies would be non-identical.

'Fraternal twins develop from two separate eggs

fertilised by two different sperm, and each baby has its own placenta. The babies may be the same sex, or a boy and a girl, but it's not possible to tell from an ultrasound scan until approximately twenty weeks into the pregnancy.'

What did it matter if they were boys or girls? she thought dismally. All she could think about was that in less than eight months' time she would be trying to care for *two* babies. That meant double lots of feeding and nappy changing, and twice the expense. How was she going to afford to bring up two children? And how on earth was she going to find the time to run Wedding Belle? It was going to be impossible. Tears filled Belle's eyes and slipped silently down her cheeks. The future was terrifying and she had never felt so alone.

Out in the waiting room, Loukas was too restless to sit on one of the uncomfortable plastic chairs and he wandered over to the window which overlooked the car park. Twins—he still couldn't quite take it in. Belle had conceived not one baby, but two—his children. Masculine pride flared inside him, but also a sense of awe. After Sadie, he had believed he would never trust another woman enough that he would want her to bear his child. But fate had given him another chance to be a father.

He thought of his parents, and he wished, as he had so often done over the years, that they were still alive. They would have been so excited to hear they were going to be grandparents of twins. His gentle, patient father would have been a wonderful *pappous*.

His throat ached and he swallowed hard. He wanted to be as good a father as his father had been to him. Despite the vast fortune he had accrued he was at heart a Greek fisherman's son and, like his father, family was more important to him than money. He wanted to create his own family—his own little dynasty on Aura, he thought, a faint smile curving his lips.

But what did Belle want? A cold hand gripped his heart as he thought back to the moment when the sonographer had announced it was twins. Belle had looked shattered. She had told him before the scan that she was struggling with the idea of being a mother, so what could she be thinking now she knew she was carrying two babies? Would she decide that she could not go ahead with the pregnancy?

Fear kicked in his stomach—a feeling of panic totally alien to him—and above all an overwhelming sense of protectiveness for his children. He needed to persuade Belle that her pregnancy was not the disaster she seemed to think, and assure her that she would have his support financially and every other way.

What he needed most right now was time to convince Belle that he would take care of her and the babies, he decided as he took his phone from his pocket and began to make a series of calls. One of the greatest benefits of being a billionaire was that people were willing to jump to his bidding and provide whatever he required if he threw enough money at them.

'I thought we were supposed to be having lunch,' Belle said dully. That was what Loukas had told her they were going to do when he had driven her away from the hospital. They had made the journey across town in silence; she had been lost in her own thoughts, and had presumed from his forbidding expression that he was still stunned by the news that she was carrying two babies. He had parked by St Katherine's Dock and led her along the walkway, but they had walked straight past two restaurants.

'We are—on here.' He stopped in front of a huge, sleek cruiser, and took her hand to guide her along the narrow gangway so that they could step on board. 'A friend of mine owns *Ocean Star*, and I've arranged for us to have lunch here so that we can have some privacy. We have a lot to discuss,' he added when Belle hesitated.

'I guess we do.' She had no idea what level of involvement Loukas intended to have with his children. He had told her he would support her, but that had been before they had learned she was expecting twins.

Her heart felt like a lead weight in her chest as she followed him down the steps to a lower deck and glanced distractedly around at the polished walnut fitments and cream velvet carpet in the opulent lounge. Her sense of unreality was growing stronger by the minute. Loukas turning up out of the blue had been a big enough shock, and the news she'd been given at the hospital had utterly floored her.

'I can't have twins,' she muttered, her brain still finding it impossible to accept.

She missed the sharp glance Loukas gave her, and was unaware that he had stiffened when he'd overheard her words. Deep, plush sofas lined the walls and she sank down onto one, feeling drained. At least she knew now why she was so exhausted all the time. Two new lives were developing inside her, and the process was robbing her of every ounce of energy.

'The crew will serve lunch in a few minutes. Until

then, can I get you a cold drink? Or would you like a cup of tea?'

Belle shook her head. 'Tea is one of the things that make me feel sick. I haven't been able to drink it for weeks.' She bit her lip, silently cursing herself for her stupidity. 'The signs that I was pregnant were there, but I didn't see them,' she said heavily.

Loukas crossed to the drinks cabinet and poured himself a whisky and soda. 'Did you really not know while you were on Aura?'

'No, I honestly had no idea. As I said, I had what I thought was a period. When my doctor told me I was pregnant it was a complete shock—but not as much of a shock as learning that I'm carrying twins.'

The sofa was soft and comfortable. Belle leaned back against the cushions and allowed her eyes to close for a few minutes, tiredness engulfing her as it so often did in the middle of the day.

Loukas studied her broodingly. His eyes lingered on the faint swell of her stomach and his insides clenched when he thought of the two precious lives she was carrying. He knew he was not thinking rationally; his actions were instinctive and born of an urgency to take Belle away to the one place he knew he could keep her and the babies safe. No doubt she would accuse him of unfair tactics when she discovered his plans, but she had fallen asleep, and with luck the *Ocean Star* would be well on its way before she awoke.

For a few seconds after she opened her eyes Belle felt disorientated, before she remembered that Loukas had brought her to have lunch on his friend's boat. She must have fallen asleep, she realised, as she glanced around the luxurious cabin. And he had carried her here, removed her shoes and put her into bed, all without her stirring. She checked her watch and felt a jolt of shock. How could she have slept for four hours?

Through the porthole she could see calm water, but when she turned her head she was startled to see water through the opposite porthole too. Puzzled, she slid out of bed—and realised with another jolt that the boat was moving. Her dress was creased, and a glance in the mirror revealed that her hair resembled a bird's nest. Her shoes were nowhere to be seen and she gave up looking for them, pulled open the cabin door and raced along to the lounge.

'Ah, you're awake.' Loukas was sitting on one of the sofas, but he put his laptop aside and stood up when he saw her. Belle's heart gave a little flip when he strolled towards her, and fragments of the dream she'd had while she had been asleep suddenly became vividly clear in her mind: erotic images of her and Loukas naked on a bed, his aroused body descending slowly onto hers. Colour flooded her cheeks. How could she be thinking of things like that at a time like this? she asked herself angrily. She had given in to her sexual craving for him once before and look where it had got her.

'You slept right through lunch. Are you hungry?'

'No.' She ignored the faint rumble from her protesting stomach. 'Loukas, what's going on? Why isn't the boat moored in the dock?' Through the bigger windows of the lounge she could see nothing but a vast expanse of water, and panic started to build inside her. 'Where are we?'

'I can't give you a precise location, but we're heading down the French coast towards Spain—*en route* to

Greece,' he said casually. 'We should arrive at Aura in two days' time. A rather longer journey than by plane, I know, but more relaxing—and an opportunity for us to discuss the future.'

Belle's temper flared at his equable reply. 'It didn't occur to you to ask me first?' she said tightly. 'We can discuss things in London. I don't want to go to Aura.'

He smiled, but his grey eyes were as hard as flint, and his implacable tone sent a chill down Belle's spine. 'I'm afraid you have no choice.'

'Don't be ridiculous. You can't kidnap me,' she said sharply. 'For one thing my brother will be expecting me back.' Guiltily she remembered how long she had slept. 'He's probably worried sick about me.'

'Dan knows where you are.' Loukas resumed his seat, looking perfectly at ease as he rested his arms along the back of the sofa and stretched his long legs out in front of him. 'He phoned your mobile while you were asleep, and I had a chat with him and assured him of my intention to accept responsibility for my children. He was stunned to hear that you are expecting twins, and agreed that it will be better for you to live at the Villa Elena rather than on a cramped houseboat—particularly as your pregnancy progresses.'

'I don't believe you,' Belle said wildly. 'Dan wouldn't have said that. He knows I need to be in London to run Wedding Belle.' Admittedly her brother had been concerned that she could not continue to live on *Saucy Sue*, but he would never have agreed to Loukas taking her to Greece without discussing it with her first. 'I don't believe you've even spoken to him.'

In reply Loukas indicated the suitcase at the far end of the lounge. 'He packed a few of your clothes and other necessities, such as your passport, and I had a courier collect your luggage from the houseboat.'

Belle sank weakly down onto the sofa. How many more shocks could she withstand? she wondered. Loukas seemed to think he could just take over her life. 'Why would Dan have done that?' she whispered. She had thought her brother was her ally.

'He wants what is best for you.'

'Taking me to Greece against my will is hardly best for me,' she snapped. 'I insist that you to take me back to London.'

'And where do you plan to live? The houseboat, with twins, is out of the question,' he added grimly.

'I intend to find a flat.' Even that would not be ideal, Belle acknowledged, but London rents were too expensive for her be able to afford a house with a garden. She sighed wearily. 'I don't know what my exact plans are yet. I hadn't got used to the idea of one baby, and to find out that there are two—' She broke off and sat twisting her fingers together in her lap while her stomach churned with worry. Her life had imploded and she couldn't imagine how she was going to juggle being the single mother of twins and working the long hours necessary to make Wedding Belle a success. 'I don't know how I'm going to manage,' she admitted shakily.

She looked so fragile. Loukas felt a curious sensation in his chest, as if his heart was being squeezed in a vice. He wanted his children more than he had ever wanted anything in his life—wanted to be a father to them and love and protect them as his father had loved him. As he stared at Belle's tense face he felt a fierce wave of protectiveness for her. It struck him that he wanted to make the worry fade from her eyes and see her smile the way she had done when they had been lovers for those few magical weeks on Aura.

'How do you feel about being pregnant, Belle?' he asked quietly.

'Shocked, disbelieving, scared.' The words spilled from her. 'I still can't believe it's happening...' She trailed off and pressed a hand to her brow, as if she could somehow hold back the jumbled thoughts in her head.

'Are you saying you don't want our babies?'

The question tore at her emotions. She stared at Loukas, and even in the midst of her turmoil she felt a tug on her heart when she studied his handsome face. Would the babies look like him? She pictured little boys with dark hair and flashing eyes, and in that moment the two little lives developing inside her became real. Pregnancy wasn't just an abstract concept; she was going to be a mother, and the realisation evoked a tremulous feeling of awe inside her.

'Of course I want them,' she said huskily. 'I hadn't planned to have children at this stage of my life, but I will love my babies.' She swallowed as an image of her mother suddenly came into her mind. She wished her mother had told her the truth about her father, Belle thought sadly, but she did not question that Gudrun had loved her. The bond between mother and daughter had been so special. Now *she* was going to be a mother, and she would give her babies the same unconditional love Gudrun had given her. 'I know things won't be easy, but I will do my best to be a good mother to them.'

Something strange was happening to Loukas. He felt a curious sensation in his chest, as if the tight bindings around his heart were slowly loosening. Belle was not like Sadie. He walked over to her and dropped down onto the sofa beside her, his body tense with resolve.

'I'm glad we both share the same desire to be parents to our children.' He knew what he had to do and accepted that he could no longer avoid commitment. He would do whatever was necessary to claim his children. 'There is only once sensible choice open to us.' He looked into her eyes and said fiercely, 'I want you to marry me.'

CHAPTER NINE

BELLE stared at Loukas incredulously. Of all the shocks she had received, his proposal was the most startling. 'You can't be serious?' she said faintly.

Her heart was pounding, and the part of her brain still functioning warned her that such violent emotional tension could not be good for the babies.

'There's no need for us to take such an extreme step,' she said sharply, trying to stem her panic. 'We can both be parents to our children without marrying. I'm sure we can act reasonably regarding access arrangements.' Even as she said the words she shuddered, picturing herself arguing with Loukas about whose turn it was to have the twins at Christmas, where they would go to school—which country they would live in. Life would be one battle after another, she thought bleakly.

He shook his head. 'Access arrangements—is that the best we can do for our children, Belle? I intend to be a proper, full-time father, not have a bit-part in their lives—only seeing them at special events or taking them to the zoo on Sunday afternoons.'

His words tugged on her emotions, but they also exacerbated her feeling of panic. 'A loveless marriage is a toxic environment in which to bring up children,' she argued. 'Believe me, I know. I witnessed my mother's unhappiness with my stepfather all my childhood.'

Loukas frowned. It was the first time Belle had ever mentioned her upbringing, and he was startled by the bitterness in her voice.

'I don't want to marry you,' she told him fiercely.

'You would rather we fought over our children, constantly vying for their affection by spoiling them with material things and making them feel that their loyalties are torn between us?' he demanded. 'What if in the future we marry other partners?' His voice hardened. 'I admit I cannot bear the idea of my children growing up with a stepfather who could not possibly love them as much as much as I will, and who might even resent them.'

Just as John had resented *her*, Belle thought, the colour draining from her face. 'That will never happen. I don't plan on ever getting married. I value my independence.'

'Then keep it,' Loukas said harshly, 'but be aware that it comes at a price. Because I *will* have my children—either through marriage or through the courts.'

Belle gasped. 'Are you saying you would seek custody of the twins?' With his money and power there was a good chance he would win any court battle.

'I hope it won't come to that. I hope that you will see sense and realise that we need to put aside what we want and give our children what they need most—two parents who are committed to bringing them up in a stable family unit.'

The worst of it was that everything Loukas was saying echoed her own belief that children had the right to be brought up by both their parents, Belle thought wearily. But *marry* him? She felt as though prison bars were closing around her. After her stifling childhood she had vowed never to give up her freedom. But if she wanted to keep her twins what choice did she have but to marry Loukas?

'I need some air,' she muttered, lurching to her feet and swaying slightly on unsteady legs.

'I don't want you to go up on deck. You haven't eaten for hours and you look like you're about to pass out,' Loukas said harshly, catching hold of her arm to prevent her from climbing the steps to the upper deck.

He was too much. She needed some time away from him to think. *'For pity's sake leave me alone!'* she cried. 'You've always got to be in control, haven't you? Everything always has to be your way.'

'Gamoto!' His black brows lowered. 'I'm simply trying to take care of you.'

'I don't need taking care of.' She fought free of his hold.

'You're so damned stubborn.' Loukas lifted a hand to rake it through his hair. He saw Belle flinch and he stilled, his hand frozen in mid-air. 'Belle? *Thee mou!* You thought I was going to *hit* you?'

He stared at her, shocked by the look of fear in her eyes. 'I have never struck a woman in my life,' he said roughly. She was so tiny, barely more than five feet tall, and she weighed next to nothing. He felt sick at the idea of someone hurting her. 'Has someone hit you in the past?' He'd like to meet whoever it was, he thought savagely. 'Who…?'

'It doesn't matter.' She didn't want to talk about it. Some memories of her childhood were best left buried.

Loukas slowly lowered his hand, his jaw tightening when he recalled how she had tensed, as if she had expected to feel a blow from him. She looked achingly vulnerable, her eyes enormous and suspiciously over-bright in her white face. He wanted to take her in his arms and reassure her that he would never hurt her, but she looked as brittle as glass and he knew she would reject any overture from him.

'Look—come and have some food.' He was careful to make it sound like a request rather than an order. 'You must be starving. The babies need you to eat,' he reminded her quietly.

His concern was for the babies, of course, not for her. But he was right. She was hungry, Belle acknowledged. He had walked to the dining table at the far end of the lounge, and after a few moments she followed him and slid into the seat he was holding out for her. Almost immediately a steward appeared to serve a first course of gazpacho.

The chilled tomato soup with its accompaniment of crispy croutons was delicious. Belle's stomach gave an inaudible rumble of appreciation and for a few minutes she concentrated on eating. Two little lives were dependent on her, and they had to be her first priority.

'Dan was telling me about his job as a fashion photographer,' Loukas murmured after the steward had replaced their soup bowls with a main course of baked chicken with a herb and lemon marinade. 'He's an interesting guy. I get the impression that the two of you are close?'

Belle knew he was deliberately steering the conversation away from the contentious issue of her pregnancy and she was grateful for the reprieve. 'We are,' she said firmly. Now that her mother was gone, Dan was her only relative. 'His real passion is to photograph wildlife. Every summer we pack up his camper van and head off for some remote moor or woodland where we have to sit patiently for hours so that he can get a shot of a rare bird or toad.' Her faint smile faded. 'I guess I won't be going with him again.' Taking two babies on a wildlife trip would be too difficult, she thought, feeling a pang of regret for the loss of her old life, where she had been free to do as she pleased. From now on the twins would always come first.

She had forgotten how charismatic and charming Loukas could be, she thought some while later, as they lingered over a dessert of pavlova with fresh raspberries and cream. He had kept the conversation light, discussing the new political thriller by an author they both enjoyed, and telling her that Larissa and Georgios were back from their honeymoon and settling into their new house in Athens. He exerted a special kind of magic over her, and although she knew it was dangerous to fall under his spell she did not seem able to stop herself.

'How about going up on deck now?' he invited, with a smile that stole her breath. He had threatened to fight for custody of her babies, she reminded herself. She would be a fool to trust him just because his smile made her heart leap.

She followed him up the steps and took a deep breath of fresh sea air. The evening sunshine was warm and the soft breeze teased her hair back from her face as she leaned against the rails at the stern of the boat. Loukas came to stand close beside her, and her senses flared as the familiar scent of his aftershave stole around her. She did not want to look at him, but her eyes were drawn to his face and lingered on the sensual curve of his mouth. Steel-grey eyes met hers and held her gaze.

'It would not be a loveless marriage,' he said quietly. For a second Belle's heart seemed to stop beating, but it resumed dully when he added, 'We will love our children. Isn't that a good enough reason for us to make a commitment to each other and to them?'

'A commitment, Loukas?' she queried huskily. 'I've seen the media reports of your playboy lifestyle and your numerous mistresses.'

He shrugged. 'My business success has made me fair game for the paparazzi, but most of those stories are untrue or exaggerated. I admit I have not lived like a monk, but I will honour my marriage vows—including forsaking all others.'

He moved before she'd realised his intention, sliding one arm around her waist to pull her up against the hard wall of his chest while his other hand tangled in her hair.

'In truth it will not be a sacrifice,' he said deeply, his eyes blazing with a feral hunger that sent a tremor through Belle. 'I wanted you from the minute I saw you, Belle, and I know you felt the chemistry between us.' His simmering gaze challenged her to deny it. 'Our physical compatibility is not in doubt.'

Her brain told her to push him away, to be strong and fight for her independence. He was too powerful, too much in control, and she was terrified of losing her freedom. But her body betrayed her, the voice of caution inside her head drowned out by the pounding beat of desire in her veins. Trapped by the compelling heat in his eyes, she watched his head lower towards her and caught her breath at the first soft brush of his lips over hers.

It seemed a lifetime since they had been lovers on Aura. She had missed him so much. Helplessly she parted her lips and heard his low groan of satisfaction as he accepted her invitation and deepened the kiss. She should not respond. He had kidnapped her and threatened to seek custody of her babies. She should hate his guts, she reminded herself angrily. But his actions had been because he was determined to be a father to his children. How could she deny her twins what she had yearned for all her childhood—a loving father?

The sensuality of his kiss was beguiling. She touched his face with trembling hands, and ran her fingers through his silky black hair. Passion was a shaky foundation on which to base a marriage, but it had taken them by storm from the very beginning and as a result she had conceived his babies. Loukas was right—they owed it to the two new lives growing inside her to make a commitment to each other, so that they could both be parents to their children.

As if he had read her thoughts he broke the kiss and lifted his head a fraction to stare intently into her eyes. 'Marry me, Belle? Let me protect you and our babies?'

His words tugged at her soul. Wasn't that what she had wanted most when she had been a child—to be protected and loved by the man she had thought was her father? She had no doubts that Loukas would love his children, and although he did not love her he had said he would be committed to their marriage. She tried to ignore the wistful ache inside her that said things should be different, and reminded herself that she might design fairy-tale wedding dresses but she had never believed in fairy tales.

'Yes.' She let out a shaky breath, feeling utterly drained from the buffeting her emotions had been subjected to in the past few hours.

Loukas tightened his arms around her, enfolding her and holding her close so that she could hear the thud of his heart beneath her ear. She knew he only cared about the babies she was carrying, but it felt good to stand like this, with his hand gently stroking her hair. Just for a little while she could kid herself that he cared about her too.

Above her head, Loukas's hard features softened a fraction, relief replacing the fierce tension that had gripped him from the moment he had discovered that Belle was pregnant. He had been denied his first child, but he *would* be a father to his twins. After Sadie, he had not expected that he would ever want to marry, but he was determined to marry Belle so that his children would be born legitimately.

He drew her closer, feeling the softness of her breasts pressed against his chest, the silkiness of her hair beneath his cheek, and felt the hot throb of desire in his groin. He would marry her to claim his babies, but having her as his wife would be no hardship, he admitted silently.

Belle stared at Loukas across the breakfast table, her frustration bubbling over. 'I need to go back to London,' she insisted. 'I can't run Wedding Belle from here. We've been on Aura for two weeks now, and although Jenny is doing her best I'm going to lose business if I don't get back to work. You agreed that I would continue to run

my company.' She reminded him of the stipulation she
had made when she had said she would marry him for
the sake of the twins.

'And *you* agreed that you would allow your office
manager to take charge of Wedding Belle until after
our wedding.' Loukas frowned. 'You know how exhausted you've been feeling. You need to take things
easy for a few weeks while the babies are developing
so quickly.'

'I feel fine,' Belle argued. 'I can't be away from
London for weeks—especially now.' Her brow creased
with worry as she recalled the phone call she'd received
from Jenny the previous day. 'There is a possibility I'm
going to lose the studio. I've had notification from the
company who own the warehouse saying that they want
to sell the building to a developer. If that happens I'll
have to look for new business premises, and the studio
space I require will cost a fortune. I can only afford to
rent the warehouse because it's old and run-down.'

Loukas studied her speculatively. 'Then perhaps you
should consider other options?'

'What do you mean?'

'It is not necessary for you to work. I'm a wealthy
man, and I can provide you and our children with a
luxurious lifestyle.'

'Are you saying you want me to give up Wedding
Belle?'

'Not necessarily, but obviously you will have to cut
back on your business commitments until after the twins
are born.'

Loukas stood up from the table, looking suave and
drop-dead gorgeous in his superbly cut charcoal-grey

suit. The breeze ruffled his dark hair and Belle's heart gave an annoying little flip.

'I have to go. Stop fretting—it's not good for the babies. You need to relax. Read a book or something.'

She was surprised he did not pat her on the head, as he would a well-behaved puppy, Belle though crossly, as she watched him stride into the house to collect his briefcase. She knew that he fussed over her and would not allow her to do anything remotely strenuous because he was concerned for the twins, but after two weeks of him taking control of every aspect of her life she felt suffocated. She missed London and her busy life running her company, and she felt lonely here on Aura while Loukas was away in Athens all day. She needed to prove to him that being pregnant did not make her an invalid—and, more importantly, she needed to take back control of her life.

Later that day Belle was beginning to wish she had not asked one of the villa staff to take her over to Kea. Determined to do something other than sit by the pool and flick through magazines all day, she had decided to explore Aura's closest neighbour. After Stavros had guided his boat into the port at Korissia, she had caught a bus to the islands' largest village of Ioulida.

It was a picturesque place, with narrow streets, white-washed houses and pretty shops and tavernas. Cars were not allowed in the town, and the sight of donkeys laden with goods made Belle feel as if she had been trans-ported back in time. But climbing the many steps up into the town in the midday heat had drained her energy, and after stopping for a rest and a cool drink at one of the bars she wearily made her way back to where she hoped she could catch the bus to Korissia.

'*Belle*! Thank the stars!'

Startled to hear her name, she turned to see Chip jogging towards her along the dusty street. He was breathing hard and she was puzzled by his tense expression. 'Chip—is everything all right?'

He exhaled heavily and reached into the pocket of his shorts for his phone. 'It is now. I've got to call Loukas and tell him I've found you.'

Her confusion grew. 'But I'm not lost. And Loukas doesn't know I'm here.'

'No, and he's been off his head ever since we discovered that you had disappeared.' Chip gave her a rather strained smile. 'Don't worry about it, Belle. Let's just get you back to Aura.'

Why hadn't it occurred to her to take a taxi back to Korissia? Belle wondered fifteen minutes later, when they arrived at the port and Chip helped her step aboard Loukas's speed boat. Chip was unnaturally quiet. His usually cheerful face was unsmiling, and when they approached Aura he grimaced as a helicopter flew overhead.

'There's Loukas.'

Belle frowned. 'Why is he back in the middle of the day?'

'He was worried about you.' Chip hesitated, as if he wanted to say more, but seemed to think better of it. 'We'd better get up to the house,' he muttered, leading the way up the cliff path.

Loukas emerged from the villa at the same moment as they walked through the gate into the garden. As he skirted the pool and strode towards her Belle saw that he was furious, his mouth compressed into a thin line and his eyes glinting like steel. Chip diplomatically disappeared into the house, and Belle found that her heart was thudding as she walked slowly forward.

'Where the hell have you been?' He did not wait for her to reply, his jaw rigid with tension. 'Why did you take off like that—without telling anyone where you were going? I've been worried sick...'

Loukas's face darkened as he recalled the phone call he'd received from Chip, saying that Belle hadn't been seen for a few hours and did not appear to be anywhere on the island. The message he'd had soon after, informing him that Stavros had taken Belle to Kea, had not lessened his frantic concern. 'You will *not* do that again.' Stress deepened his accent. 'I forbid you to leave Aura without my prior knowledge.'

He snatched a harsh breath and became aware of the stunned expression on Belle's face. The silence between them simmered before she spoke in a tightly controlled voice.

'Forbid?' She shook her head fiercely. 'You have no right to forbid me to do anything. You don't own me, Loukas. We're not even married yet and you're trying to take over my life.' Panic filled her—the sensation of prison bars closing in on her. 'I won't allow you to control me. If this is what my life as your wife is going to be like—not being allowed to breathe without your permission—then I've changed my mind and I won't marry you.'

His eyes blazed as he caught hold of her arm to prevent her from walking past him. 'You cannot change your mind. I won't allow it.' She *had* to marry him. He needed to keep her here on Aura so that he could protect her and his children. Loukas closed his eyes as the image of his father crumpling to the floor, blood pumping from the bullet hole in his stomach, filled his mind. The world was a dangerous place, but here on his private island he could keep Belle safe.

'I'm not trying to control you,' he said harshly. 'But in some things you must do as I say.'

'And if I don't?' Anger gave Belle the strength to wrench herself free of his hold. Fear churned inside her. She would not allow Loukas to dominate her as her stepfather had done. 'What then?' she demanded. 'Will you use physical force to make me obey you? That's what John used to do. I spent my whole childhood being scared of a bully.' Her vision suddenly blurred and she dashed the tears away with the back of her hand. 'I refuse to live my life being scared any more.'

She whirled away from him and raced towards the house. He caught up with her in seconds and turned her round to face him. *'Let me go.'*

'Thee mou, Belle, calm down.' Loukas stared down at her tear-stained face and felt a pain as if he had been kicked in his gut. She was trembling, her eyes wide with fear, and he wanted to haul her close. He exhaled deeply. 'I would never harm you in any way. Surely you know that?' It hurt him to think that she was afraid of him. His hand shook slightly as he lifted it to smooth her hair back from her face, and gradually he felt her tension lessen a little. 'Let's sit down,' he said gruffly, indicating the two sun loungers by the edge of the pool. 'We need to talk.'

Belle's legs gave way. She sank down onto a cushioned lounger and darted Loukas a wary glance.

He raked a hand through his hair. 'Who is John?

Belle?' he prompted softly when she did not reply. 'We are going to be married. There should not be secrets between us.'

Secrets were not a good thing, she acknowledged, thinking of the secret her mother had kept from her. She let out a shaky breath. 'He's my stepfather, but I grew up believing he was my real father. It's complicated,' she said ruefully when Loukas frowned. 'My mother was married to John, but she had an affair and fell pregnant with me. John threatened to claim custody of Dan, who is his real son, if Mum left him for her lover. And so she stayed with him, and I grew up believing that John was my dad.'

'But he treated you badly?' Cold rage settled in the pit of Loukas's stomach as he remembered the look of fear on Belle's face when she had thought he was about to strike her.

She nodded. 'Yes. But he never hit me in front of Mum or Dan, and I never told them. Children don't,' she said painfully. 'I believed I was bad in some way and deserved his anger. John was a hard man, an army sergeant-major, and at home he demanded absolute obedience. But even though I tried to be good I was never able to please him. I used to wonder why he didn't love me.'

She bit her lip. 'My mother grew up in an orphanage, and I think it was important for her to create a family unit for me and Dan. I guess that's why she stayed with John even though it was a miserable marriage. When she died three years ago John told me the truth, and then his dislike of me made sense. I was another man's daughter—a living reminder that Mum had been unfaithful to him. I haven't had any contact with him since her funeral.'

'What about your biological father—do you have a relationship with him?'

'No, I don't know who he is. Mum never told me anything.' She hesitated, finding it hard to reveal her private thoughts and yet somehow compelled to confide in Loukas. 'Since I found out that my real father is a faceless stranger I will never meet I've often felt that I'm not a complete person. There's a whole side to me that I will never know. Maybe I have a family somewhere that I will never be part of.'

She looked away from Loukas and stared out over the crystal-clear pool and the sapphire-blue sea beyond. 'That's why I agreed to marry you,' she whispered. 'I want my babies to grow up with their father so that they feel whole, and assured of who they are—confident that they are loved.'

'Don't ever doubt it,' Loukas said deeply. 'I will love my children as my parents loved me.' As he would have loved his first child, if only he had been given the chance, he thought darkly.

He studied Belle's delicate features and felt a surge of impotent fury against her bully of a stepfather. He understood now why her independence was so important to her, and what a huge leap of faith it must have been for her to agree to marry him. Unlike Sadie, she was willing to put the needs of her babies before what she wanted. The revelation struck him at that moment that he did not want her to regard marriage to him as a sacrifice of her freedom. Her happiness was important to him, and he wanted her to be happy with him.

'I don't wish to control you,' he said quietly. 'All I want to do is keep you and our babies safe.'

His emotive words tugged on Belle's heart. 'I suppose I should have mentioned to one of the staff that I was leaving Aura for a couple of hours,' she acknowledged. 'I just needed to get away for a while. And, really, what harm could come to me on Kea?'

'Details of our engagement have been reported world-wide. I am a very wealthy man, and as my fiancée you are a possible target for kidnappers,' Loukas explained in a strained tone. 'Naturally I would pay whatever ransom was demanded for you, but the trauma of being snatched and held perhaps in unpleasant circumstances could result in you suffering a miscarriage.' He leaned forward and took both her hands in his. 'From now on I want you to promise that you will never go anywhere without either me or Chip. He is a trained bodyguard, and if for some reason I'm not with you he will ensure your safety.'

The possibility of being kidnapped by criminals had never crossed Belle's mind, and she instinctively placed her hand protectively over her stomach. It had happened before around the Mediterranean—she had read of sev-eral cases where a member of a wealthy family had been snatched, and a huge ransom demanded. 'Is that why you are so protective of Larissa?' she asked shakily.

He nodded. 'Perhaps I am over-protective, but I spent my youth living in a part of New York where violent crime was an everyday occurrence. I witnessed things that I will never forget.' Loukas's voice roughened with emotion. He never spoke about his past, preferring to bury it deep in his subconscious, but he needed to try and explain to Belle why he liked to be in control of every situation.

'My father was murdered before my eyes,' he said harshly. 'I couldn't save him—couldn't protect him from the gang, high on drugs and wielding a gun, who burst into our shop demanding money from the till. When my father tried to reason with them, they shot him at point-blank range.'

Belle's heart stood still. 'Oh, Loukas.' She did not know what to say, and instinctively clasped his hand. No wonder he was so determined to protect the family he had left—and his children who were yet to be born. How could she blame him for wanting to keep his babies safe, and her safe too while she was carrying them?

He stared down at their entwined fingers and then lifted his eyes to her face. 'I don't want you to think of Aura as your prison, Belle. I want it to be our home, where we will bring up the twins in a safe environment.'

She nodded. 'I understand now why that is so important to you. And I love Aura. I don't have a problem with being here.'

'Does that mean that I am the problem?' He trapped her gaze, an emotion she could not define flaring in his eyes. 'I am not a man like your stepfather,' he said intently. 'I swear I will never hurt you.'

He closed the gap between them and slanted his mouth over hers, his kiss slow and sweet and so achingly gentle that tears gathered in Belle's eyes. She wound her arms around his neck when he lifted her, and her heart beat faster when he carried her into the house and up the stairs, heading purposefully in the direction of her bedroom.

Since Loukas had brought her to Aura they had occupied separate rooms. It had seemed right when their relationship was so fragile. She had been relieved that he had not expected her to share his bed, knowing that she would not be able to hide her vulnerability from him if he made love to her. So much had happened since the heady days of their affair. They had parted, and were only together again because she was pregnant.

But now, as he laid her on the bed and kissed her with growing passion, she felt a shaft of piercing longing to lie with him and make love with him. He was the father of her babies and she felt a fundamental connection with him that she knew would remain with her for the rest of her life.

She sighed with pleasure when he deepened the kiss, and cupped his face between her hands, stroking the slight roughness of his jaw. This was where she wanted to be, in his arms, with his lips trailing a moist path down her throat and his hand gently caressing her breast. She remembered how his voice had cracked when he had spoken of his tragic past, and her heart ached for him. Loukas was a survivor, who had fought his way out of poverty to become hugely wealthy and successful, but beneath his tough exterior she had glimpsed the boy who had been emotionally scarred by his father's murder. Instinctively she held him close as tenderness swept through her.

Loukas had lost count of the nights he had lain awake, his body aching with desire for Belle, or how often he had dreamed of the softness of her skin and the delicate fragrance of her perfume. Now she was here in his arms, and the pulse beating frantically at the base of her throat told him she shared his urgent need to rediscover the passion that had been at the heart of their relationship during their affair.

But the situation was different now. They were not carefree lovers. The only reason Belle was here on Aura was because she was pregnant with his babies. He lifted his head and felt his heart clench when she smiled at him. She was so beautiful, but unlike every other woman he had ever known her loveliness went right down to her heart. It would be easier if she was shallow and superficial, as so many of his past mistresses had been, he thought grimly, for then he could take her to bed and enjoy meaningless sex with her.

But if he made love to Belle it would not be meaningless. He stiffened as the realisation slid into his brain, and he fiercely rejected the idea. He did not want to need her. He did not want her to mean anything to him. Life had taught him that it was easier not to care, because that way you didn't get hurt.

Belle wondered why Loukas suddenly seemed so tense. She wished he would kiss her again, but to her intense disappointment he sat up and raked a hand through his hair. She didn't understand what was wrong, why he would not look at her. Moments ago she had been sure he was going to make love to her, but now, as he leapt up from the bed and strode towards the door, she felt hurt that he clearly could not wait to get away from her.

'You must be tired after your trip to Kea,' he said abruptly. 'Get some rest and I'll see you at dinner.'

His rejection felt like a slap in the face. He had said that their physical compatibility was not in doubt, but as far as Belle could see it was non-existent. Maybe he no longer desired her, she thought miserably. Her body was already changing shape due to her pregnancy, and perhaps he found her unattractive.

Once again she was swamped with doubts about their forthcoming marriage. During their affair sex had been a vital part of their relationship, but if Loukas was no longer attracted to her would he look elsewhere to satisfy his high sex drive? And would she be trapped in a loveless marriage for the sake of her children like her mother had been? The future suddenly seemed frighteningly uncertain.

CHAPTER TEN

BELLE ended the call on her mobile phone and closed her eyes for a moment, feeling the sting of tears behind her eyelids. When she opened them again she saw Loukas standing in the doorway of her room.

'I came to see if you're ready. The party starts at seven and we really should be going.' He frowned when he saw the bright glitter in her eyes. '*Thee mou*! What's wrong?' he demanded urgently, walking swiftly towards her. 'Belle, what is it?'

'That call was from Jenny, my office manager. The warehouse has been sold and we've been given a month's notice to vacate the studio,' she told him in a choked voice. 'I've been researching other possible premises for Wedding Belle on the internet, but so far I haven't found anywhere that is suitable and affordable. And there are so many other things to consider. I'll have to have stationery and business cards reprinted once I have a new address, and there are costs involved in moving and setting up somewhere else.' She rubbed her brow wearily. 'I'll have to go back to London straight after the wedding to sort things out.'

Loukas stiffened. 'You still intend to continue running your company, then?'

'Yes, of course. Nothing would make me give up Wedding Belle. You have no idea how important it is to me,' she said as Loukas frowned. 'Starting up my own dress design business is the one thing I've done that I'm really proud of. John was convinced I would fail. He told me I wasn't talented enough to succeed. But my mother had faith in me.' She bit her lip. 'Mum died while I was in the process of setting up Wedding Belle, but I know she would have been proud of me.'

She brushed her hand over her wet lashes and did not see the curious expression that crossed Loukas's face, was unaware that her visible distress felt like a knife through his heart. 'I guess it sounds silly, but running my own business makes me feel like I'm *someone*,' she confessed. 'I don't know who my father is, but Wedding Belle gives me an identity.'

The knife in Loukas's chest gouged deeper. 'Of course you are someone,' he told her roughly. He slid his fingers beneath her chin and tilted her face to his, brushing away her tears with an unsteady hand. 'You are a beautiful, talented young woman, soon to be the mother of my children, and tomorrow I will be proud to make you my wife. I did not realise how much Wedding Belle means to you,' he continued in strained voice. 'I'm sure your mother would be immensely proud of you.' He hesitated. 'Have you considered establishing your company in Greece? I could help you find a studio in Athens.'

'It's an idea,' Belle said slowly. 'I have been wondering how I will manage to work in London once the babies are born. But I don't speak Greek yet, and it seems rather daunting to set up the company in a foreign country.'

'Greece will be your home,' he reminded her.

'I suppose it will.' She stared at Loukas. 'I know you have your doubts that I can combine being a mother to the twins with running a business, but I'm sure I can do it. I'll give serious thought to the idea of looking for a studio in Athens.'

The party was a charity fund-raising event to be held in the opulent surroundings of one of Athens's most prestigious five star hotels, and the guest list included several government ministers and a sprinkling of celebrities.

'I think you should sit down for a while,' Loukas murmured as he steered Belle off the dance floor. 'You've been on your feet all evening, and I don't want you to get too tired.'

'I'm not at all tired,' she protested, wishing she was still in his arms, their bodies moulded together as they drifted in time to the music. She knew the sense of closeness she had felt with him while they were dancing was an illusion, but for a while she had been able to pretend that they were like a normal couple who were in love and looking forward to their wedding.

'I can't believe how much my pregnancy is showing,' she said ruefully when she caught sight of her reflection in one of the ballroom mirrors. She knew she was showing early because she was carrying twins, but it was daunting to imagine how big she would be by the end of her pregnancy.

Following the direction of her gaze, Loukas glimpsed Belle's expression. 'You look beautiful tonight,' he assured her softly, desire flaring inside him as his eyes roamed over her. He knew the cornflower-blue ballgown was one of her own creations; its full skirt disguised the faint swell of her stomach and the strapless bodice cupped her breasts, displaying their new fullness and tempting him to free them from their silk covering and caress her soft flesh with his hands and mouth. His body stirred into urgent life and he fought to bring his libido under control as the hostess of the party approached them.

'I hope you are both enjoying the evening?' Gaea Angelis greeted them warmly. 'Loukas, I believe Zeno wants to discuss a new project with you in the library.'

He glanced at Belle. 'Do you mind if I excuse myself for a few minutes? Sit down, hmm? You shouldn't stand for too long.'

'He's very protective, isn't he?' Gaea commented when Loukas walked away. 'And tomorrow is your wedding—are you excited, Belle?'

Apprehensive was a better description of how she felt, Belle thought to herself. She did not doubt that becoming Loukas's wife was the best thing to do for her babies, but there was no escaping the fact that it was a marriage of convenience—for Loukas. He wanted his children, and that was his only reason for marrying her.

She forced a bright smile. 'Yes, I can't wait.'

'It's good to see Loukas so content. We never thought he would settle down after his relationship with Sadie ended so abruptly.'

Belle stiffened, and queried in a carefully casual tone. 'Was Sadie the woman he hoped to marry?'

'Yes, Sadie Blaine—I expect you've heard of her. She's a top Broadway star, and now her film success has made her the hottest thing in Hollywood.'

Belle was stunned by Gaea's revelation. Sadie Blaine was an American actress, singer and dancer—an international star who, as well as being phenomenally talented, was stunningly beautiful. The news that Loukas had been engaged to her was astounding.

'Loukas was clearly devastated by the split, but he refused to talk about it,' Gaea explained. 'But now he is going to marry you, and I'm sure you will both be very happy together.'

Would they be happy? Belle wondered later, as she stared out of the helicopter window at the bright lights of Athens which blazed in the night sky. Would Loukas be happy with her—or would he always secretly wish that he had married the woman from his past whom Larissa had once told her had been the love of his life?

They were both silent during the journey back to Aura. Loukas seemed lost in his thoughts, and Belle felt sick with jealousy when she pictured him with gorgeous Sadie Blaine. When the helicopter had landed and they were walking up to the villa she could not hold back the question that had dominated her mind since her conversation with Gaea Angelis.

'Why didn't you tell me you were once engaged to Sadie Blaine?'

He gave her a sharp look. 'I suppose Gaea was gossiping?' He shrugged, 'I didn't mention it because it isn't important.'

'But you were in love with her?'

He was silent for so long that Belle thought he was not going to answer. 'Yes,' he said finally, in a voice that warned her he did not want to continue with the discussion.

Belle bit her lip, self-doubt surging through her. 'I'm nothing like Sadie. I mean, she's stunningly beautiful and a world-famous star. I saw her in a show at the

London Palladium last year and she was electrifying. She's every man's fantasy woman.' While in a few months from now *she* would be fat and ungainly, her stomach swollen with the babies and her ankles swollen from water retention, Belle thought miserably.

'I agree you are nothing like Sadie.' Loukas's harsh voice scraped across her raw emotions. 'But she is in the past. You are the woman I am going to marry.'

But only because she was pregnant. The painful truth swirled inside Belle's head. No doubt he would eventually have married some beautiful, cultured socialite who would have made him a far more suitable wife than her.

She trailed into the villa behind him, haunted by the same feeling of inadequacy that she had so often felt during her childhood. John had made her feel as though she was not good enough to deserve his love, and now she was convinced that Loukas regarded her as second best compared to the famous star he had wanted to marry. Was that the reason he had walked away from her last night? she wondered bleakly. Had he not made love to her because he still desired his beautiful ex?

'Shall we go up to the roof terrace for a while?' Loukas suggested. It was a routine they had fallen into since Belle had returned to Aura, and she had come to treasure the evenings they spent beneath the stars, chatting, or simply sitting in companionable silence. But tonight her emotions felt too raw for her to risk being alone with him.

'I'm going to bed,' she said shortly. 'It's going to be a busy day tomorrow.' She hurried up the stairs, but he followed her and caught up with her outside her bedroom door.

'What's wrong, *agape*?'

The gentle endearment tugged at her heart. 'Nothing,' she muttered. She tried to move away from him, but he slid his hand beneath her chin, his eyes darkening when he saw the shimmer of tears she could not hold back. 'My life was all mapped out, but now everything has changed,' she burst out. 'I don't know what's going to happen to Wedding Belle now that I've lost the studio. I'm scared that I'm not going to be a good mother—I don't know anything about babies.' She stared at him, feeling the familiar weakness in her limbs when she studied his handsome face. 'And tonight I've discovered that you probably wish you were marrying someone else,' she finished bleakly.

'That's not true,' Loukas said fiercely, feeling his insides turn over as a tear slipped down her cheek. 'You are the woman I want to marry, Belle.' He swallowed, aware that there were so many things he needed to tell her. He could no longer fight the feelings inside him—could no longer deny his need for her. Her vulnerability tugged at his soul, and he wanted to kiss away the hurt he could see in her eyes.

He pulled her against him, and as their bodies met his tenuous hold on his self-control shattered and he wrapped his arms around her, his big body shaking with an intensity of longing that overwhelmed him. He knew they should talk, but right now all he wanted to do was lose himself in the sweetness of her body and forget everything but the pleasure of making love to her.

He lowered his head and captured her mouth, feeling the little tremor that shook her as she hesitantly parted her lips and kissed him back. He could never have enough of her, and he tasted her again and again, until his desire for her spiralled out of control and he swept her up into his arms, shouldering open the door and carrying her across her bedroom to set her down by the bed.

Belle caught her breath as Loukas trailed fierce kisses down her throat and over the slopes of her breasts. His urgency thrilled her and dismissed her doubts that he did not find her attractive. His hands were clumsy as he tugged the zip of her dress down her spine, and he gave a harsh groan when her breasts spilled into his hands. With feverish haste he pushed her dress over her hips, so that it pooled at her feet, but the sudden exposure of her body evoked her uncertainty once more and she tried to cover her stomach.

'My body is changing,' she whispered, catching her lower lip with her teeth.

'Of course it is—and pregnancy makes you lovelier than ever.' His eyes glittered with feral hunger, but tenderness made his voice shake as he gently tugged her hands down. 'Do you have any idea what it does to me to know that my babies are inside you?' he said thickly. He stroked the rounded fullness of her breasts with a reverence that made Belle tremble, and then sank to his knees and pressed his lips to the soft swell of her stomach.

Molten heat flooded between Belle's thighs when he pulled down her knickers and trailed his mouth over the triangle of blonde curls and finally to the moist heart of her femininity, his tongue exploring her with delicate precision so that pleasure rippled through her and her knees sagged. He caught her to him and laid her on the bed, ripping off his clothes with frantic haste before he stretched out next to her.

'Belle *mou*.' His breath whispered across the rosy tips of her breasts, and she gasped when he anointed each one in turn, the flick of his tongue over her acutely sensitive nipples causing her to arch her hips in mute supplication.

Desire pounded in Loukas's veins, but the need to be gentle made him temper his passion, and he eased her thighs apart and aroused her with his fingers until she cried out. Only then did he enter her with exquisite care, groaning when her muscles enveloped him in velvet, tightening around him so that each thrust drove him closer to the brink. But he forced himself to wait, to slow his pace so that she caught his rhythm. Only when he saw her eyes darken and heard the soft gasps that told him she was hovering on the edge did he allow his control to splinter, and he drove into her and felt her convulse around him at the same moment that he spilled into her.

Afterwards he held her close, her head resting on his chest while their breathing slowed. Through the open window Belle could hear the gentle lap of the waves on the shore, as rhythmic and comforting as the steady beat of Loukas's heart beneath her ear, and she fell asleep feeling safe and secure in his arms.

The first thing Belle saw when she opened her eyes was a single red rose on the pillow beside her. She smiled, a tremulous feeling of happiness unfurling inside her like the petals of a rosebud coming into bloom. It was going to be all right.

Nothing had really changed, she reminded herself. Loukas was still marrying her because she was carrying his babies, but last night he had proved that he desired her, and he had made love to her with such tender passion that she felt sure they could make their marriage work. He might not love her, but friendship and respect were a good basis for their relationship, and maybe, in time, he would come to care for her.

The wedding was only to be a small affair, and Loukas had managed to rush through the paperwork necessary for them to marry. Larissa and Georgios were to attend, as well as the household staff, but Dan was on a photoshoot in New Zealand and had promised to visit Aura as soon as he could.

'*Ise panemorfi*—very beautiful,' Maria proclaimed after she had helped Belle into her wedding dress.

'I hope Loukas thinks so,' Belle murmured, as she stared at the reflection of her ivory silk dress with its fitted bodice and full skirt. She had never expected that she would make her own bridal gown—had never planned to get married—and now that it was almost time for the wedding she could not help feeling nervous. Loukas was not a bully like John Townsend, she reassured herself. His gentle lovemaking last night had convinced her that she would not be trapped in an unhappy relationship like her mother had been.

Her mobile rang and she answered it, smiling when her office manager explained that she was calling to wish her luck. 'Where are you going for your honeymoon?' Jenny asked.

'I'm not. I'm hoping to come back to London as soon as possible to sort out new premises for Wedding Belle. I don't suppose you were able to persuade the new owners

of the warehouse to give us more time before we have
to move out?'

'I'm afraid not. The executive I spoke to from
Poseidon Developments said that plans are already un-
derway to convert the warehouse into luxury flats.'

'Poseidon Developments—are you sure that's the
name of the new owners?' Belle said slowly.

'Yes—funny name for a company, isn't it?' Jenny
laughed. 'Wasn't Poseidon a Greek god?'

'He certainly was.'

A cold feeling settled in the pit of Belle's stomach
as she said goodbye to Jenny. Loukas owned a sub-
sidiary company called Poseidon. During one of her
conversations with Chip while Loukas was at work,
he had mentioned that Christakis Holdings was made
up of a number of different companies which Loukas
had called after Greek gods. 'Poseidon Developments,
Apollo Group, Zeus Financial—but not Eros,' Chip had
laughed. 'The boss balked at calling one of his businesses after the god of love.'

It must be a coincidence, she told herself. After all,
why would Loukas want to buy an old warehouse in
London? Admittedly it was probably a good site for
development, but he knew that she had her studio there,
and he had been unexpectedly sympathetic when she
had learned that the warehouse had been sold. If he had
bought it he would have told her, wouldn't he?

She tried to put it out of her mind, but she felt a
curious sense of dread in the pit of her stomach as she
walked down the stairs to meet Chip, who was to escort
her to the church. It was true that Loukas had never
been enthusiastic about her decision to continue running
Wedding Belle after they were married. But last night

she had been surprised and pleased when he had offered to help her find new premises in Athens.

But she wouldn't need a new studio if the London warehouse had not been sold, her brain pointed out. And relocating her business to Greece was not ideal, because she would have to build up her clientele from scratch. She bit her lip. Nothing made sense. If Loukas really was the new owner of the warehouse surely he would have allowed her to keep her studio—*unless he had hoped that she would give up Wedding Belle.*

'You look stunning, Belle,' Chip greeted her, his face creased into a wide smile as he presented her with a bouquet of red roses. 'The boss said to be sure to give you these.' He paused, and then added softly, 'You light up his life, you know.'

His words tore at her heart. She had believed she knew Loukas, but now she was afraid she did not know him at all.

'All set?' Chip proffered his arm. 'We'd better get over to the church.'

She hesitated, gnawing on her bottom lip. 'Chip, did you say that Loukas owns a company called Poseidon Developments?'

'That's right. He has various companies under the umbrella of Christakis Holdings.' Chip looked at her curiously. 'Why?'

'No reason,' she said shakily.

She gripped the roses tightly as she entered the cool, cloistered quiet of the church. It took a few seconds for her eyes to adjust to the dimness after the brilliant sunlight outside, and as she looked ahead to Loukas's tall figure waiting at the altar panic swept through her. She trusted him, didn't she? The fact that he owned a company with the same name as the new owners of the warehouse *must* be a coincidence. But what if it wasn't? What if he had deliberately made it difficult for her to carry on with Wedding Belle?

Her steps faltered. She was aware of Chip's puzzled glance but she could not go on. She could not marry Loukas when there were so many questions in her mind.

He must have wondered why it was taking her so long to walk the short distance to the altar, because he'd turned his head. She stared into his eyes, searching for some sign that the despair in her heart was unfounded.

'Tell me that the Poseidon Developments who have bought the warehouse in London and given me notice to leave my studio is not the Poseidon Developments owned by you,' she pleaded.

He stiffened, and stood so still that it was as if he had been carved from granite. The nerve flicking in his cheek was the only indication of the fierce tension that gripped him.

Disbelief turned to agonising reality. 'Oh, no!' she whispered, shaking her head, as if she could dismiss the terrible truth that she could see in his shocked gaze. Her heart felt as though it had been sliced open, and she was surprised that she was not bleeding down the front of her white wedding dress. *'Oh, no!'* she bit her lip so hard that she tasted blood. 'Why did you do it?'

'Belle…' He jerked forward and she immediately stepped backwards, holding out the bouquet of roses like a shield.

'You wanted me to give up Wedding Belle, didn't you? But why?' she asked desperately. 'I made it clear that I would always put the babies first.' She drew a shuddering breath, pain and anger ripping through her. 'I thought you were different than John. I thought I could trust you. But you are just like him. You want your own way, and you don't care who you hurt as long as you are in control.'

'*No*—it's not like that.' He took another step towards her and suddenly Belle's control snapped. She could see Larissa's startled face, Chip frowning, trying to understand what was going on. But nothing mattered except that she should get away from Loukas before he saw how much he had hurt her.

'*Get away from me!*' she yelled at him. 'You can keep your goddamn roses.' She threw the bouquet with such force that it hit him in the chest. Red rose petals scattered on the floor of the church like a parody of confetti, like drops of blood from her broken heart. There was a terrible silence, but she did not wait around to hear it as she turned and fled back down the aisle, emerging from the church blinded by tears and running as if her life depended on it—away from Loukas.

The path led down to the beach, and he caught up with her as she stumbled along the sand. 'Belle—*please*, you have to listen to me.' He was pale beneath his tan and his face was haggard, but she was unmoved, too hurting inside to care.

'Why should I? You're deceitful and a liar, and no way on earth am I going to marry you.'

He jerked his head back as if she had slapped him. 'You *have* to,' he said hoarsely. 'You have to marry me, Belle.'

She lifted her chin, scorn blazing in her eyes, determined not to reveal that she was breaking apart inside.

'Why? For the babies' sake? So that you can be their father? Maybe they will be better off with no father than one who wants to control everyone around him.'

He put a hand across his eyes, and Belle felt her heart jolt with shock when she saw that his cheeks were wet. 'You don't mean that.' His voice shook and he swallowed hard. 'I don't want to control you—I just want to take care of you. And you have to marry me—not for the babies, not for any reason other than…I love you.'

She swayed as the blood drained from her face, and squeezed her eyes shut as if she could make him go away. 'How can you say that after what you've done?'

He walked towards her, his eyes intent on her face. 'Because it's the truth,' he said fiercely. 'I love you, and I will keep saying it over and over, until the end of time if necessary, until you believe me.'

'How can I believe you?' she asked him, brushing away her tears with a shaking hand. 'You knew that if I lost my studio I would struggle to find new premises for Wedding Belle and that I might even have to give up my business.'

'Yes, I knew. That's why I did it.' He saw the confusion in her eyes and his face twisted. 'I wanted to keep you on Aura, where you would be safe—you and the babies. If I could, I would wrap you in cotton wool,' he said thickly. 'I didn't want you to spend time in London, away from me. I wanted you with me always, so that I could protect you. I will never forget how my father died. I have seen how dangerous the world can be and I couldn't bear the idea of something happening to you.' His voice cracked. 'I know I wasn't thinking rationally, but I lost both my parents in terrible circumstances, and then my child. I could not bear to lose you too.'

He raked a hand through his hair. 'I know what I did was wrong. When I saw how much Wedding Belle meant to you I realised what a terrible thing I had done and immediately instructed my lawyers to sign over the deeds of the warehouse to you. You'll be able to expand your studio, and if you decide to set up a sister company in Athens I have already found suitable premises. It will be your choice as to where you base your company, and I will support any decision you make.'

Belle was struggling to take it all in. 'You lost a child?' she said faintly. 'What happened? Who…?'

'Three years ago Sadie was pregnant with my baby,' he said harshly. 'But she didn't want the baby and she had an abortion.' He saw the shock in Belle's eyes. 'I need to tell you about Sadie,' he said heavily. 'Will you hear me out, Belle?'

She stared at him, and her heart turned over at the haunted expression in his eyes. 'Yes,' she whispered. 'Tell me about her.'

He reached for her hand, and after a second she slipped her fingers in his and allowed him to lead her down to the shore, where lazy waves rippled onto the sand.

'I first met Sadie when my family moved to New York,' he said harshly. 'Back then she was Sadie Kapowski—Blaine is her stage name. Her parents were Polish immigrants, mine were Greek.' He grimaced. 'The Kapowskis were the only people I knew who were poorer than us. Sadie shared my determination to leave the rough streets of the Bronx and make a better life, and we were both given a chance when she won a place at a performing arts school and I was awarded a college scholarship.'

He stared out towards the sea, remembering his father out on his fishing boat. 'But then my father was killed, and my mother died not long after, and I had to leave college to take care of Larissa. The responsibility of bringing up a child when I was so young myself was tough,' he admitted. 'Being with Sadie was the only good thing in my life. But she was focused on making it as a dancer and ended our relationship. It hurt like hell,' he admitted roughly. 'But I understood how much she wanted fame and a career on the stage, and so we went our separate ways and I put all my energy into the property development business I'd started.'

Belle frowned. 'I thought you said Sadie was pregnant with your child three years ago?'

Loukas nodded. 'When we met again we had both realised our dreams and built successful careers. I think one of the reasons I was drawn to her was because she had known my parents—she was a link with them, and the only person who shared my memories of them because Larissa had been so young when they died.'

Belle understood why that must have been important to him, and how alone he must have felt since he had lost his parents.

'So you fell in love with her just as you had done years before?' she murmured, hating herself for feeling jealous. After losing his parents in such tragic circumstances Loukas had deserved to find happiness.

'I believed we were destined to spend the rest of our lives together. I had achieved greater success and wealth than I had ever dreamed of, but something was missing from my life. Meeting Sadie again felt like the final piece of the jigsaw was in place. I fell for her hard, and

I thought she loved me. But Sadie always had her own agenda,' he said darkly.

'We had been lovers for almost a year. Sadie had moved into my apartment in Manhattan and I'd bought Aura and commissioned an architect to design a house that I hoped would become a family home for us once we were married.' Loukas's jaw tightened. 'One evening Sadie collapsed during a performance and was rushed to hospital. The news that she was pregnant was a shock to me, but not to her. She admitted she had known for several days that she had conceived my child. I was over the moon at the prospect of being a father. I couldn't wait to create my own family and to love my child just as my parents had loved me. But without my knowledge Sadie checked into a clinic and made sure there was no baby.'

Belle let out a shaky breath. 'I'm so sorry.' The words seemed inadequate. She placed her hand on the slight swell of her stomach where her babies were nestled inside her and thought emotively of the child Loukas had lost. 'Why did she—?' She broke off, unable to say the words.

'Her career,' he answered harshly. 'Sadie had made it to the top. She was an acclaimed Broadway star. But she was terrified of her fame slipping. To her mind, having a baby would have compromised her career. She could not bear the thought of losing her figure and refused to take even a few months away from the stage in case some rising star took her place. And she admitted that the idea of living on a tiny Greek island and bringing up children was her idea of hell,' he finished bitterly.

So many things made sense now, Belle thought heavily. Loukas must have been so hurt by Sadie's cruel betrayal. Instinctively, she held his hand against her stomach. 'I used to think that Wedding Belle was all that mattered to me—until I fell pregnant. I had no idea that I would feel like this.' She could not put into words the feeling of protectiveness and love she felt for her unborn twins.

'Sadie ripped my heart out, and I swore that I would never fall in love again.' Loukas paused and then said quietly, 'And then I met you. I saw a tiny, beautiful blonde standing on the quayside on Kea and my heart stopped,' he said softly.

Her eyes widened. 'You tried to bribe me to go back to England!'

'You bet I did. I knew I was in trouble right from the start, and I was sure that if I took you to Aura my life would never be the same again.'

Belle's heart was beating too fast and she took a ragged breath. 'I felt like that too,' she admitted. 'When I stepped onto your boat I had a strange feeling that everything would be changed from that moment. And it was. We had a few weeks of great sex, and that should have been the end. But I fell pregnant,' she said flatly.

'I agree the sex was incredible, but was that really all we had?' he asked softly.

She thought back to the heady days of their affair. Their desire for one another had been explosive, but as well as passion there had been companionship, laughter, a sense of closeness that she had never felt with another human being. Afterwards, when she was back in London, she had told herself she had imagined all those things.

'You walked away from me at the airport without looking back.' She had cried for the entire four-hour flight back to England, and the memory caused tears to clog her throat.

'It took every ounce of willpower I possessed not to turn back and snatch you into my arms. It took three weeks of missing you like hell while I was in South Africa to make me see sense—and then I came back for you.' He paused, and then said quietly, 'When I first found you on the *Saucy Sue* I was not aware that you were pregnant.'

She had forgotten that. With everything that happened afterwards she had not thought about the reason for his unexpected visit. 'You told me you were in London on business,' she said warily.

'I lied. I came because I realised that I had fallen in love with you.'

When Belle made no response, simply stared at him with huge, stunned eyes, he continued. 'I was going to ask you if we could be lovers—not just a sexual affair, but a committed relationship where we could get to know each other properly and share more than just our physical desire. I planned to woo you with romantic dinners and flowers—the works. I guess it sounds corny, but I wanted to make you happy, and I hoped to persuade you to fall in love with me.'

She could not believe it was true—dared not believe the fierce emotion blazing in his eyes. 'Do you really love me?' she whispered.

He stroked her hair back from her face, his hand shaking as much as his voice. 'With all my heart and soul,' he vowed deeply. 'Is it so hard to believe, *glikia mou*?'

Her mind flew back across the years and she was a little girl again, wearing a new dress for her birthday and excitedly running to show her father. *'Do I look pretty, Daddy?'*

Cold eyes looking her up and down. John's voice sneering. *'You really are an unappealing child.'*

The excitement had drained away, her birthday ruined. There must be something very bad about her if her own father did not love her.

She snapped back to the present and stared at Loukas's handsome face, feeling as though her heart was going to burst. 'It's just that I have wanted you to love me for so long,' she admitted raggedly, tears overspilling and sliding down her cheeks. 'The weeks we spent together were the happiest of my life. I love you, Loukas.'

'Belle…' he groaned, as he snatched her into his arms. 'I need you in my life, my beautiful Belle,' he confessed, his voice aching with emotion. 'You make me complete.'

He kissed her with such gentle reverence that she could not hold back her tears. 'I thought I would be lonely for ever,' she whispered. 'I love you so much.'

He lifted his head and stared into her eyes, his love for her filling every pore in his body. And then he dropped to his knees in front of her and reached into his jacket. 'I have wanted to give you this for a long time,' he told her as he took her hand and slipped the ring onto her finger. 'Will you come back to the church with me, Belle, and be my wife, my lover, the love of my life for eternity?'

The sapphire on her finger reflected the colour of the sea, and the diamonds surrounding it glistened as brightly as her tears. But they were tears of joy, and she smiled softly at him as she knelt on the sand and wrapped her arms around his neck.

'I will,' she vowed softly.

EPILOGUE

SEVEN months later their twins were born by Caesarean section. Belle had been disappointed when her obstetrician had advised against a natural birth because she was small and her babies were a good size, but Loukas was secretly relieved. Having watched a film on childbirth at one of the antenatal classes, he had become frantic with worry that Belle would suffer a long and painful labour.

'I feel a failure,' she had told him when she was wheeled into the operating theatre, clutching his hand as he walked beside the trolley.

'How can that be, when you are the most amazing woman in the world?' he'd reassured her. She had coped with the demands of pregnancy without a word of complaint, even though he knew that she had found the last weeks exhausting. He would have done anything to take her place, but had had to be content with rubbing her aching back and truthfully assuring her that he found her pregnant shape utterly beautiful.

But when her son was placed in her arms, followed a few minutes later by her daughter, Belle forgot that she had hoped to bring them into the world surrounded by scented candles and the sound of a recorded whale song.

'They're here safely and that's all that matters,' she whispered as she and Loukas stood over the two cribs and watched their newborn infants sleeping.

They named them Petros and Anna, after Loukas's parents, and took them back to Aura when they were two weeks old. 'When he's older I'll take him fishing, like my father did me,' Loukas promised, cradling his son in his arms.

'And Anna too,' Belle said, looking down at her tiny daughter's pretty face. 'Don't forget her.' She knew that Greek men often favoured their sons, but Loukas understood her fears and was quick to reassure her.

'Of course Anna too—we'll all go. We're a family.' He slipped his arm around Belle's waist and felt his heart overflow as they stood together, holding their babies. 'I love our children with all my heart,' he said deeply. 'But you, Mrs Christakis, are the love of my life.'

* * * * *

CLASSIC

EXTRA

COMING NEXT MONTH from Harlequin Presents®
AVAILABLE MAY 29, 2012

#3065 A SECRET DISGRACE
Penny Jordan

#3066 THE SHEIKH'S HEIR
The Santina Crown
Sharon Kendrick

#3067 A VOW OF OBLIGATION
Marriage By Command
Lynne Graham

#3068 THE FORBIDDEN FERRARA
Sarah Morgan

#3069 NOT FIT FOR A KING?
A Royal Scandal
Jane Porter

#3070 THE REPLACEMENT WIFE
Caitlin Crews

COMING NEXT MONTH from Harlequin Presents® EXTRA
AVAILABLE JUNE 12, 2012

#201 UNDONE BY HIS TOUCH
Dark-Hearted Tycoons
Annie West

#202 STEPPING OUT OF THE SHADOWS
Dark-Hearted Tycoons
Robyn Donald

#203 REDEMPTION OF A HOLLYWOOD STARLET
Good Girls in Disgrace!
Kimberly Lang

#204 INNOCENT 'TIL PROVEN OTHERWISE
Good Girls in Disgrace!
Amy Andrews

You can find more information on upcoming Harlequin®
titles, free excerpts and more at www.Harlequin.com.

HPECNM0512

REQUEST YOUR FREE BOOKS!

◆Harlequin *Presents*

PASSION GUARANTEED SEDUCTION

2 FREE NOVELS PLUS
2 FREE GIFTS!

YES! Please send me 2 FREE Harlequin Presents® novels and my 2 FREE gifts (gifts are worth about $10). After receiving them, if I don't wish to receive any more books, I can return the shipping statement marked "cancel." If I don't cancel, I will receive 6 brand-new novels every month and be billed just $4.30 per book in the U.S. or $4.99 per book in Canada. That's a saving of at least 14% off the cover price! It's quite a bargain! Shipping and handling is just 50¢ per book in the U.S. and 75¢ per book in Canada.* I understand that accepting the 2 free books and gifts places me under no obligation to buy anything. I can always return a shipment and cancel at any time. Even if I never buy another book, the two free books and gifts are mine to keep forever.

106/306 HDN FERQ

Name	(PLEASE PRINT)	

Address		Apt. #

City	State/Prov.	Zip/Postal Code

Signature (if under 18, a parent or guardian must sign)

Mail to the **Reader Service:**
IN U.S.A.: P.O. Box 1867, Buffalo, NY 14240-1867
IN CANADA: P.O. Box 609, Fort Erie, Ontario L2A 5X3

Not valid for current subscribers to Harlequin Presents books.

**Are you a current subscriber to Harlequin Presents books
and want to receive the larger-print edition?
Call 1-800-873-8635 or visit www.ReaderService.com.**

* Terms and prices subject to change without notice. Prices do not include applicable taxes. Sales tax applicable in N.Y. Canadian residents will be charged applicable taxes. Offer not valid in Quebec. This offer is limited to one order per household. All orders subject to credit approval. Credit or debit balances in a customer's account(s) may be offset by any other outstanding balance owed by or to the customer. Please allow 4 to 6 weeks for delivery. Offer available while quantities last.

Your Privacy—The Reader Service is committed to protecting your privacy. Our Privacy Policy is available online at www.ReaderService.com or upon request from the Reader Service.

We make a portion of our mailing list available to reputable third parties that offer products we believe may interest you. If you prefer that we not exchange your name with third parties, or if you wish to clarify or modify your communication preferences, please visit us at www.ReaderService.com/consumerschoice or write to us at Reader Service Preference Service, P.O. Box 9062, Buffalo, NY 14269. Include your complete name and address.

HP11B

Harlequin Romance

A touching new duet from fan-favorite author

SUSAN MEIER

First Time **DADS!**

When millionaire CEO Max Montgomery spots
Kate Hunter-Montgomery—the wife he's never forgotten—
back in town with a daughter who looks just like him, he's
determined to win her back. But can this savvy business tycoon
convince Kate to trust him a second time with her heart?

Find out this June in

THE TYCOON'S SECRET DAUGHTER

And look for book 2 coming this August!

NANNY FOR THE MILLIONAIRE'S TWINS

Saddle up with Harlequin® series books this summer
and find a cowboy for every mood!

A Ferrara would never sit down at a Baracchi table for fear of being poisoned.

Fia had no idea why Santo was here. He didn't know.

He *couldn't* know.

"*Buona sera*, Fia."

A deep male voice came from the doorway, and she turned. The crazy thing was, she didn't know his voice. But she knew his eyes and they were looking at her now—two dark pools of dangerous black. They gleamed bright with intelligence and hard with ruthless purpose. They were the eyes of a man who thrived in a cutthroat business environment. A man who knew what he wanted and wasn't afraid to go after it. They were the same eyes that had glittered into hers in the darkness three years before as they'd ripped each other's clothes and slaked a fierce hunger.

He was exactly the same. Still the same "born to rule" Ferrara self-confidence; the same innate sophistication, polished until it shone bright as the paintwork of his Lamborghini.

She wanted him to go to hell and stay there.

He was her biggest mistake.

And judging from the cold, cynical glint in his eye, he considered her to be his.

"Well, this is a surprise. The Ferrara brothers don't usually step down from their ivory tower to mingle with us mortals. Checking out the competition?" She adopted her most businesslike tone, while all the time her anxiety was rising and the questions were pounding through her head.

Did he know?

Had he found out?

A faint smile touched his mouth and the movement distracted her. There was an almost deadly beauty in the sensual curve of those lips. Everything about the man was dark and sexual, as if he'd been designed for the express purpose of drawing women to their doom. If rumor were correct, he did that with appalling frequency.

Fia wasn't fooled by his apparently relaxed pose or his deceptively mild tone.

Santo Ferrara was the most dangerous man she'd ever met.

Will Santo discover Fia's secret?

Find out in THE FORBIDDEN FERRARA
by USA TODAY bestselling author Sarah Morgan,
available this June from Harlequin Presents®!

SPECIAL EDITION

Life, Love and Family

USA TODAY bestselling author

Marie Ferrarella

enchants readers in

ONCE UPON A MATCHMAKER

Micah Muldare's aunt is worried that her nephew is going to wind up alone in his old age…but this matchmaking mama has just the thing! When Micah finds himself accused of theft, defense lawyer Tracy Ryan agrees to help him as a favor to his aunt, but soon finds herself drawn to more than just his case. Will Micah open up his heart and realize Tracy is his match?

Available June 2012

Saddle up with Harlequin® series books this summer and find a cowboy for every mood!

Available wherever books are sold.

www.Harlequin.com

HSE65674